BENNY AND PENNY
IN
LIGHTS OUT!

GEOFFREY HAYES

BENNY AND PENNY
IN
LIGHTS OUT!

A **BIG**, mean dinosaur came and *ate* everyone up!

A TOON BOOK BY

GEOFFREY HAYES

ABDO Spotlight

For Pascual—a little night music!

Editorial Director: **FRANÇOISE MOULY** · Book Design: **FRANÇOISE MOULY**

GEOFFREY HAYES' artwork was drawn in colored pencil.

ABDOPUBLISHING.COM

Reinforced library bound edition published in 2016 by Spotlight, a division of ABDO
PO Box 398166, Minneapolis, Minnesota 55439. Spotlight produces high-quality reinforced library bound
editions for schools and libraries. Published by agreement with TOON Books.

Printed in the United States of America, North Mankato, Minnesota.
092015
012016

THIS BOOK CONTAINS
RECYCLED MATERIALS

A
TOON
BOOK

www.**TOON-BOOKS**.com

LIBRARY OF CONGRESS CATALOGING-IN-PUBLICATION DATA

This book was previously cataloged with the following information:

Hayes, Geoffrey.
 Benny and Penny in Lights out! : a TOON Book / by Geoffrey Hayes.
 p. cm.
Summary: At bedtime two mouse siblings take turns telling stories and calming night fears.
ISBN 978-1-935179-20-7
1. Graphic novels. [1. Graphic novels. 2. Bedtime--Fiction. 3. Brothers and sisters--Fiction. 4. Mice--Fiction.] I.
Title. II. Title: Lights out!
PZ7.7.H39Bc 2012
741.5'973--dc23

          2011050927

ISBN 978-1-61479-424-0 (reinforced library bound edition)

ABDO
Spotlight
A Division of ABDO
abdopublishing.com

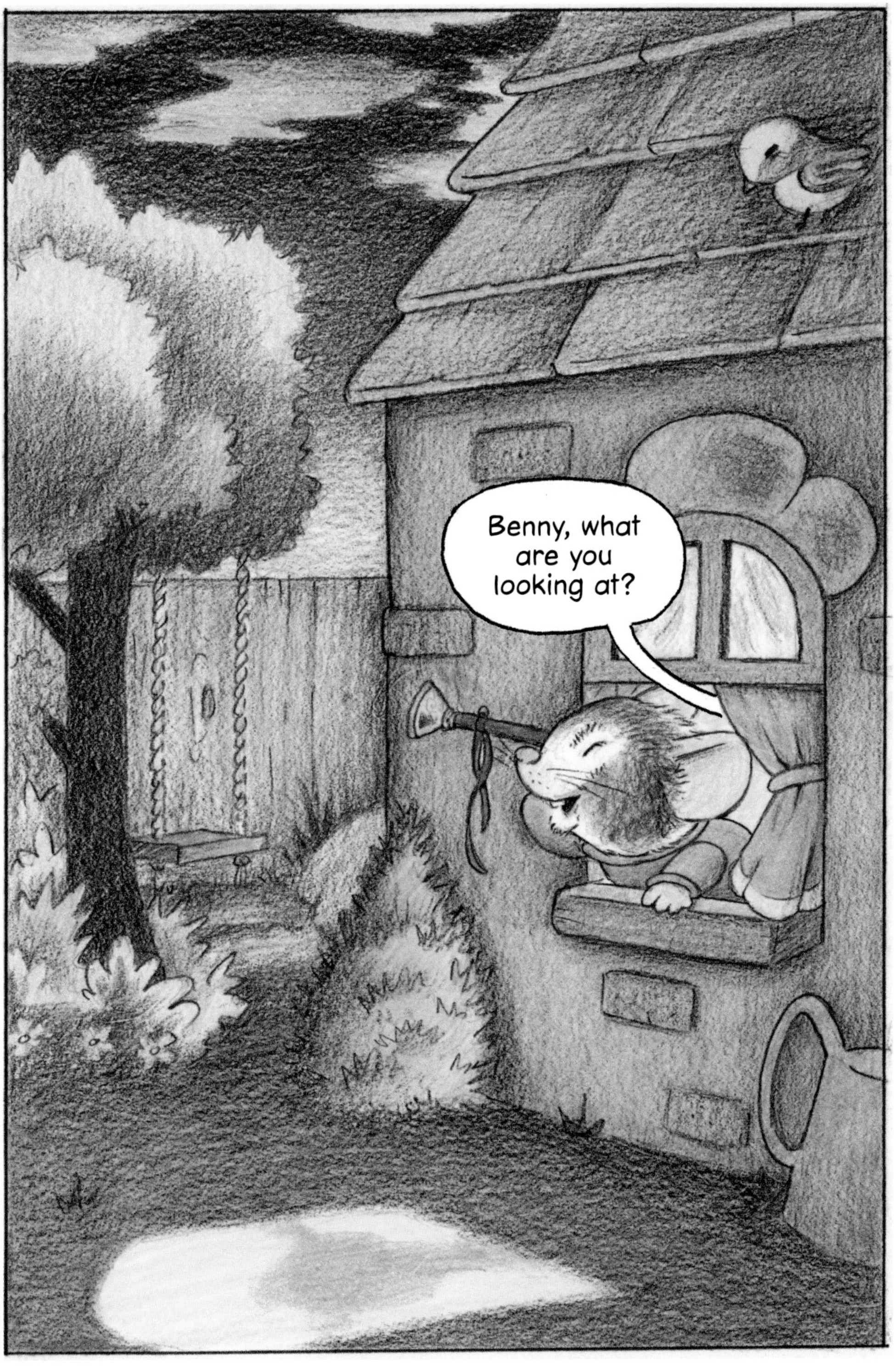
Benny, what are you looking at?

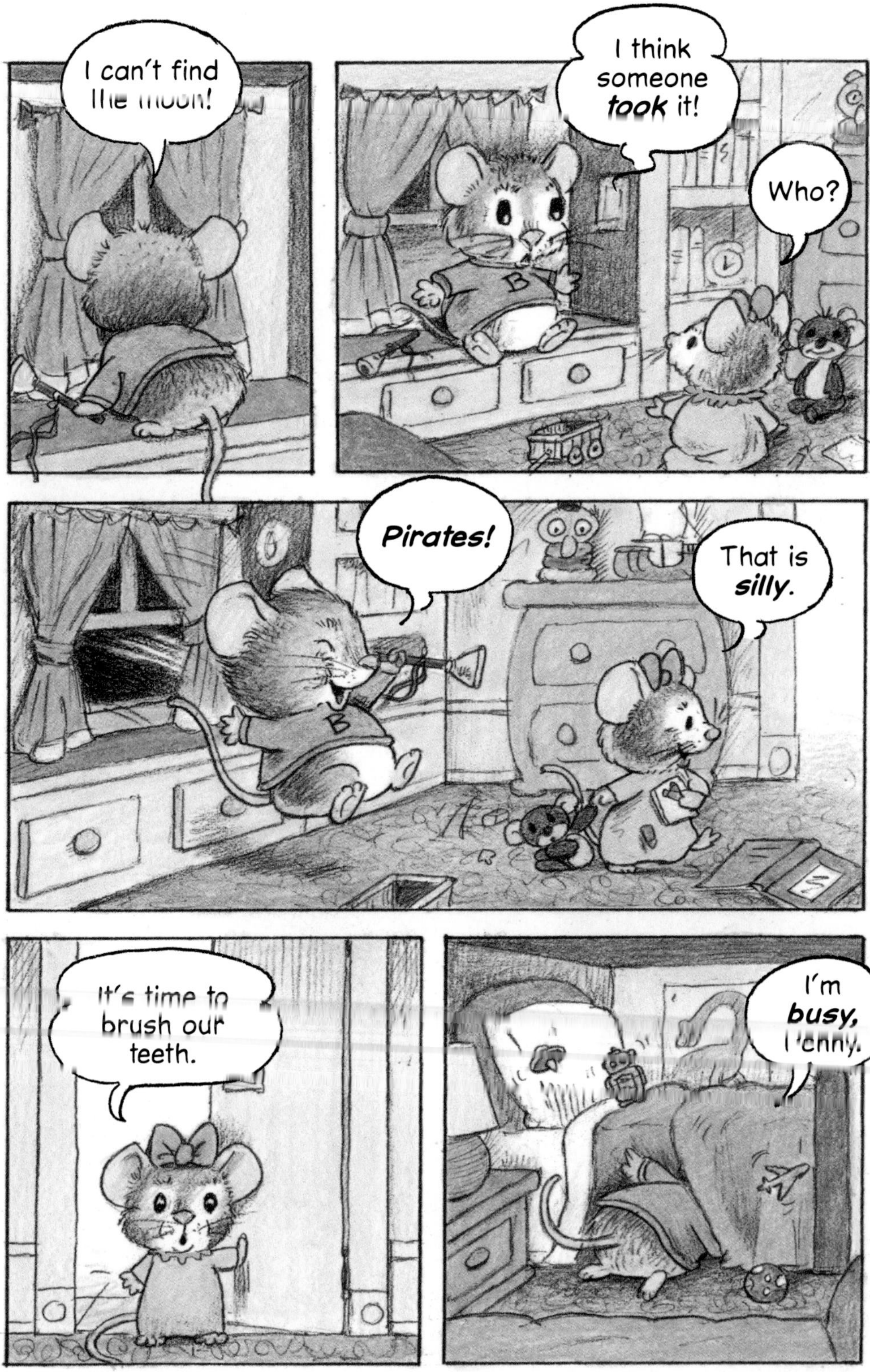
I can't find the moon!
I think someone ***took*** it!
Who?
Pirates!
That is ***silly***.
It's time to brush our teeth.
I'm ***busy,*** Penny.

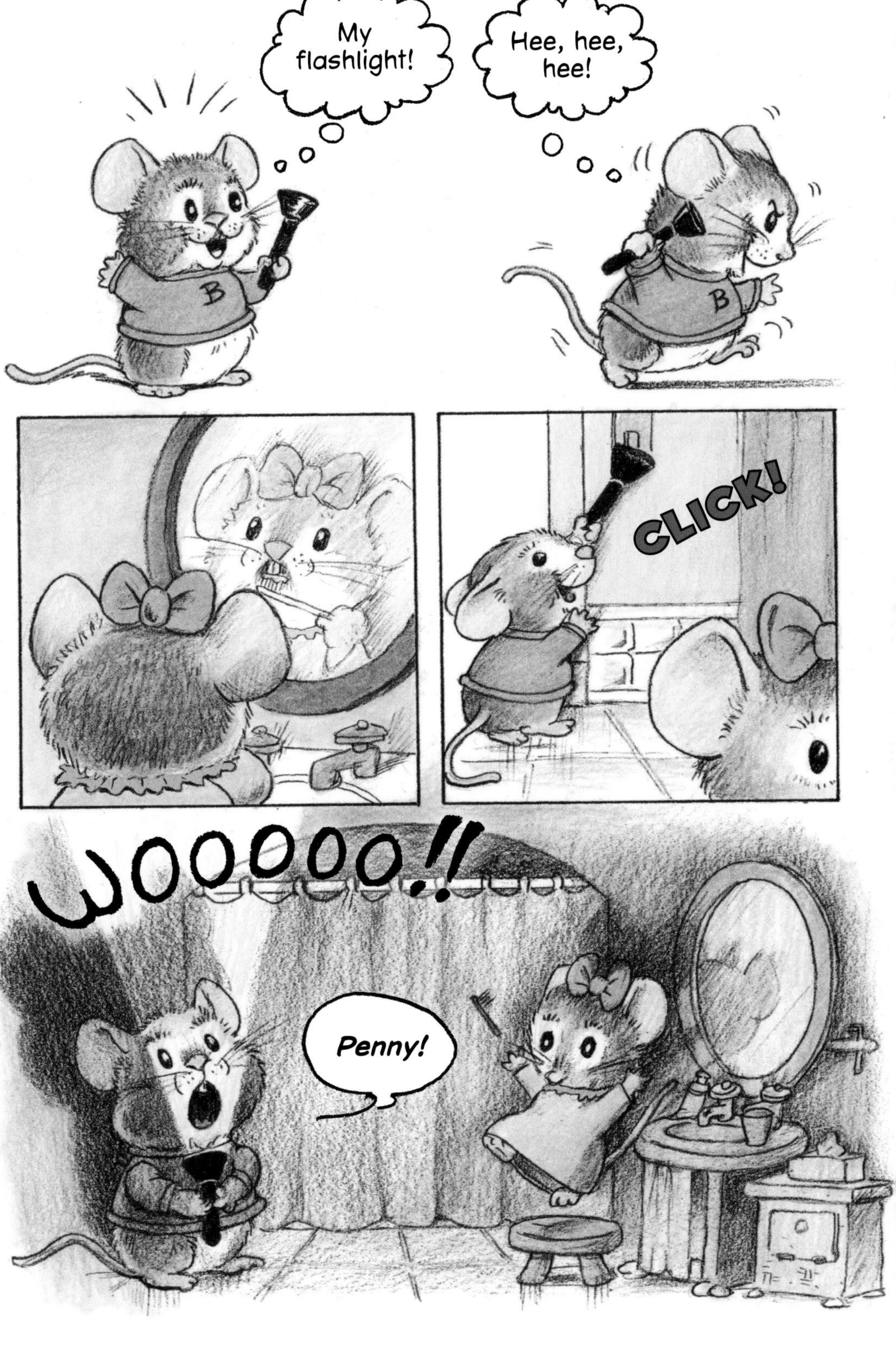
My flashlight!
Hee, hee, hee!
CLICK!
WOOOOO!!
Penny!

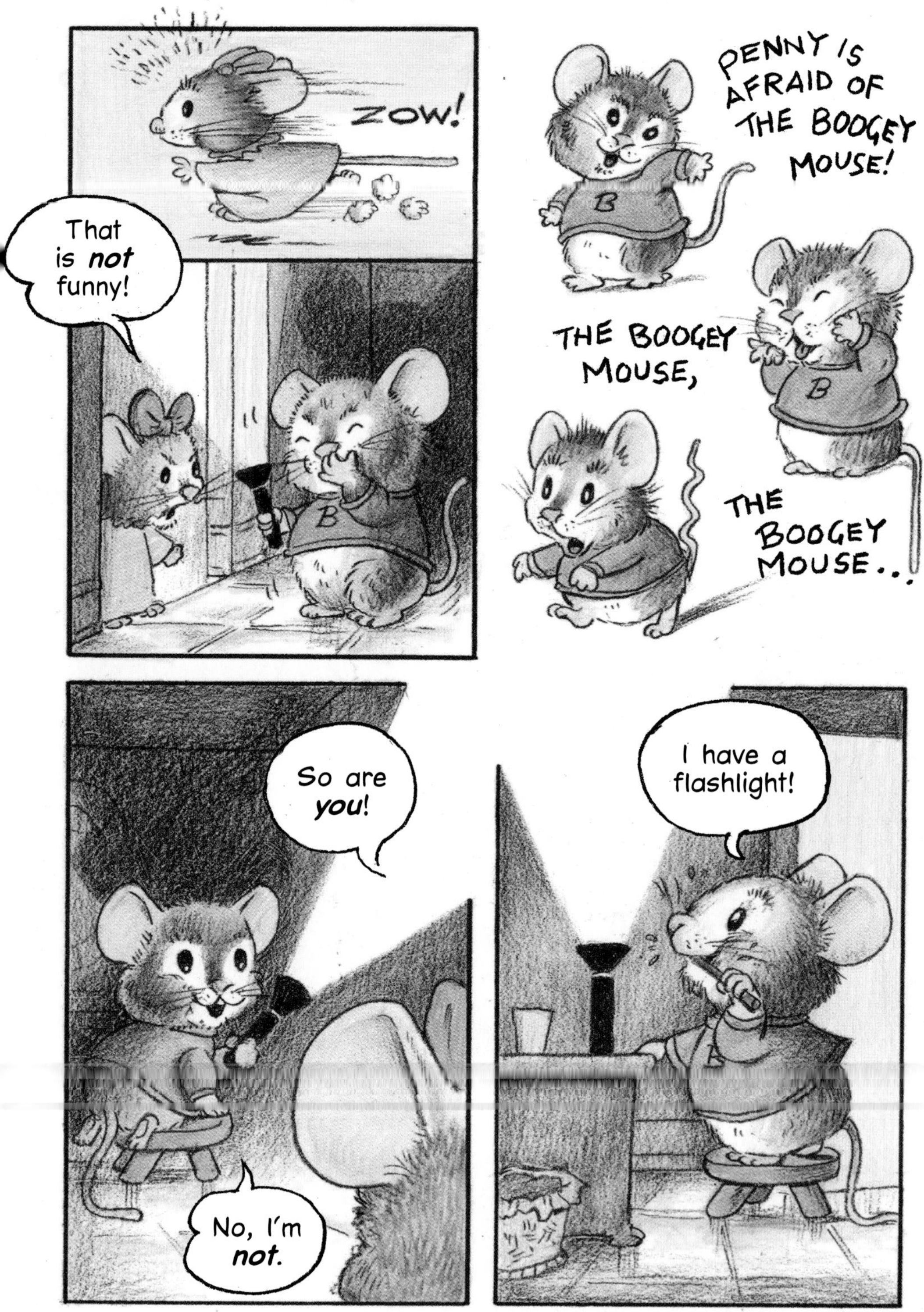
ZOW!
That is not funny!
PENNY IS AFRAID OF THE BOOGEY MOUSE!
THE BOOGEY MOUSE,
THE BOOGEY MOUSE...
So are you!
No, I'm not.
I have a flashlight!

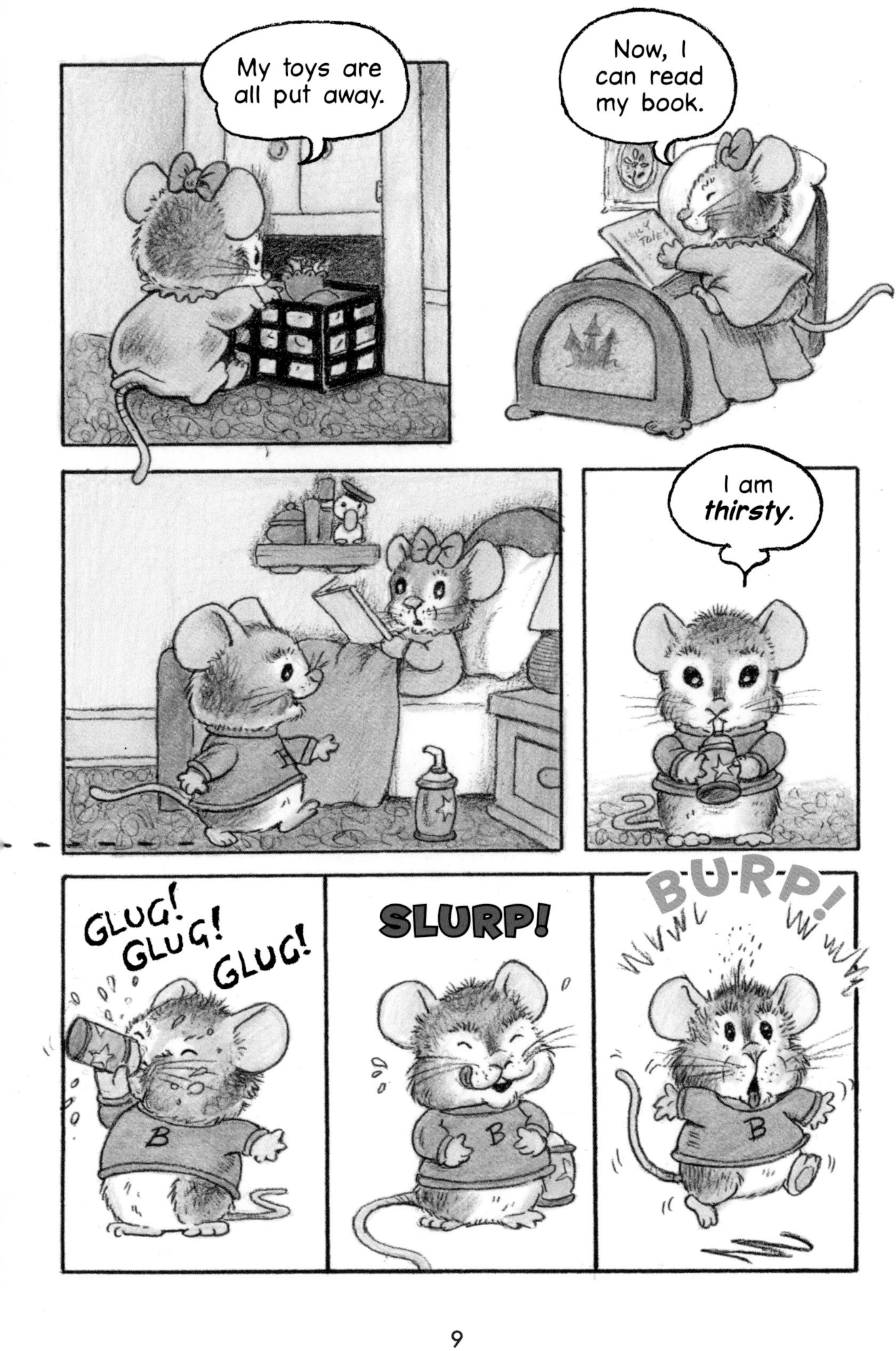
My toys are all put away.
Now, I can read my book.
I am *thirsty*.
GLUG! GLUG! GLUG!
SLURP!
BURP!

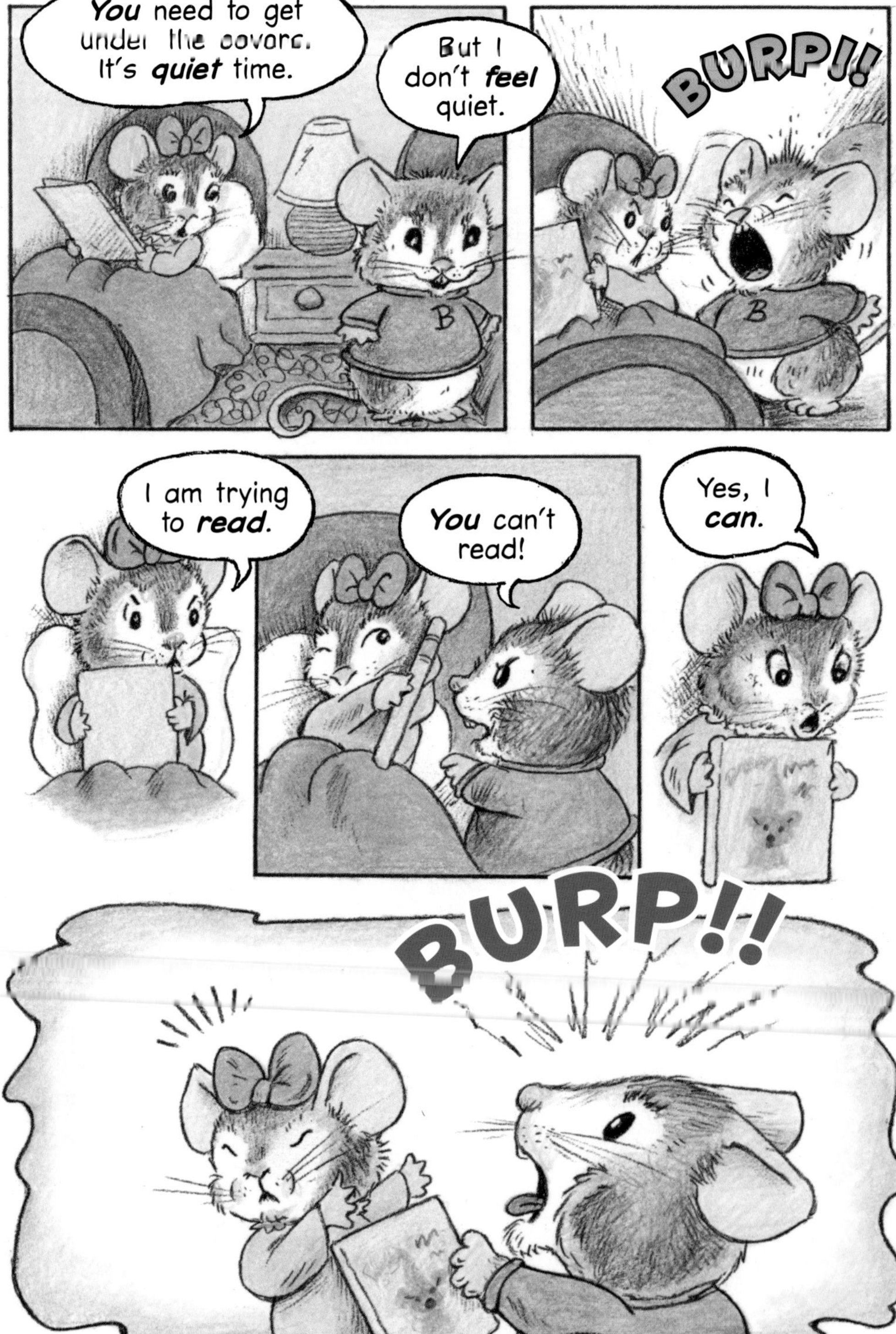
You need to get under the covers. It's quiet time.
But I don't feel quiet.
BURP!!
I am trying to read.
You can't read!
Yes, I can.
BURP!!

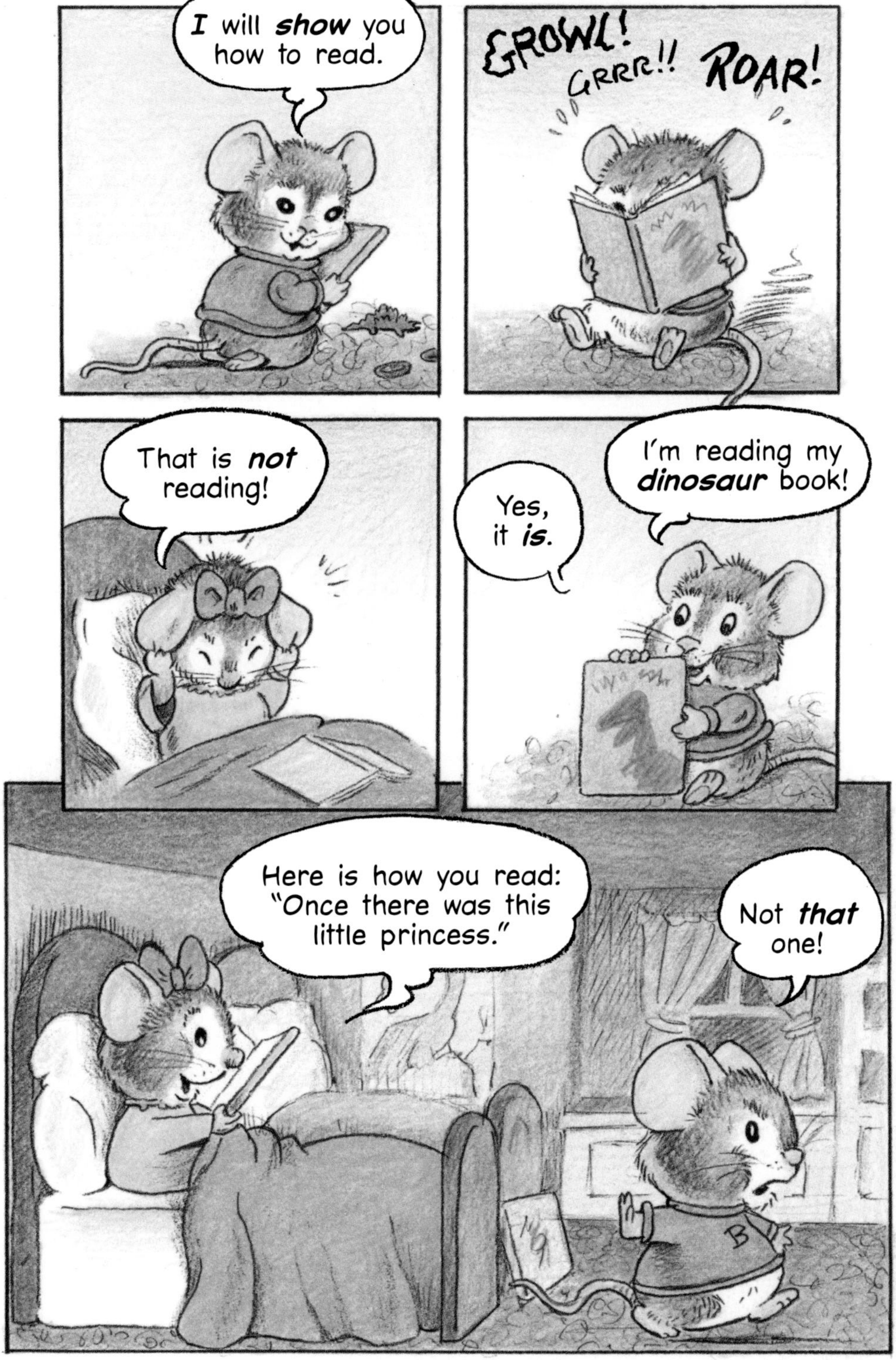
I will ***show*** you how to read.
GROWL!
GRRR!!
ROAR!
That is ***not*** reading!
Yes, it ***is***.
I'm reading my ***dinosaur*** book!
Here is how you read: "Once there was this little princess."
Not ***that*** one!

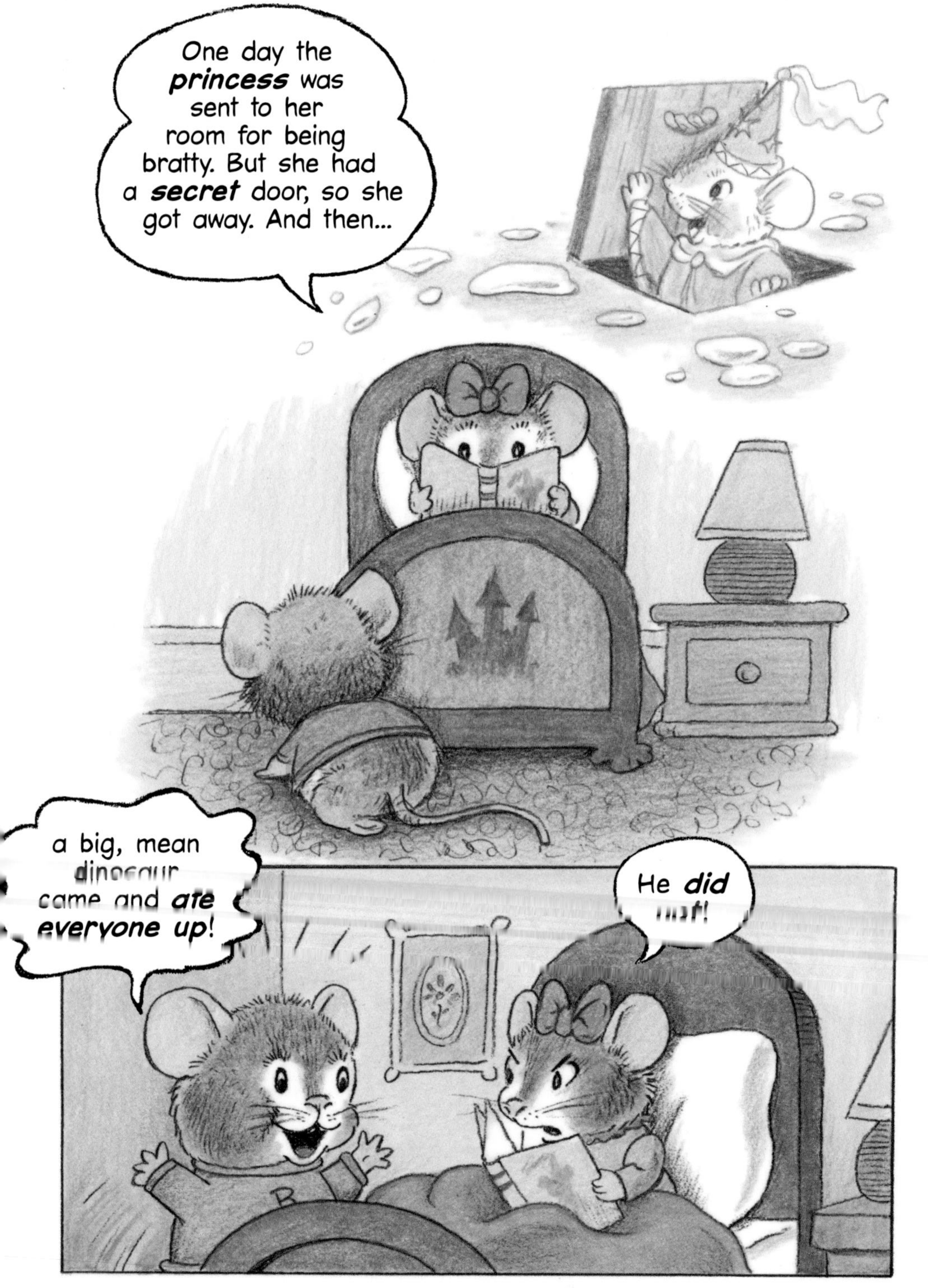
One day the ***princess*** was sent to her room for being bratty. But she had a ***secret*** door, so she got away. And then...
a big, mean dinosaur came and ***ate everyone up***!
He ***did***

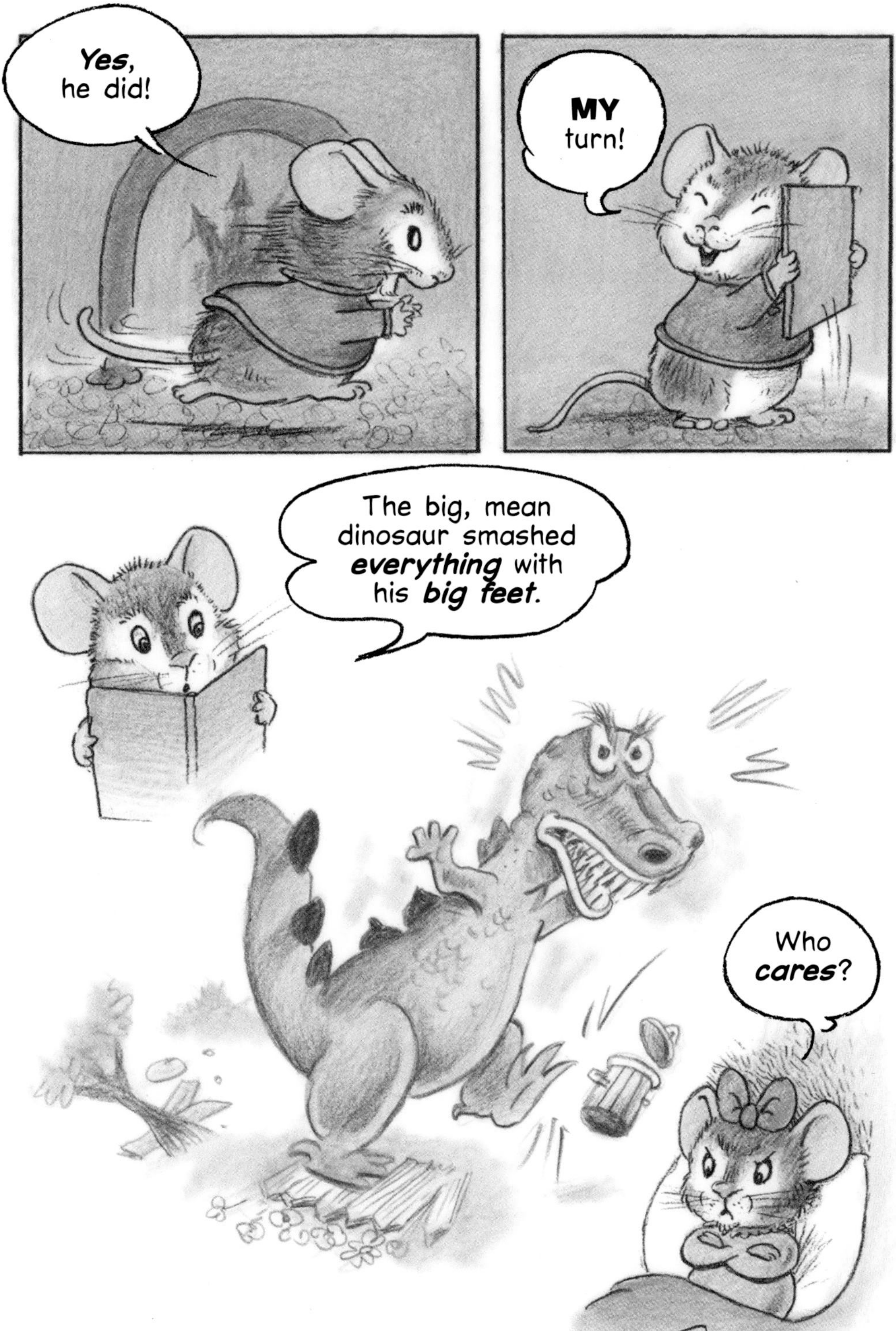
Yes, he did!
MY turn!
The big, mean dinosaur smashed ***everything*** with his ***big feet***.
Who ***cares***?

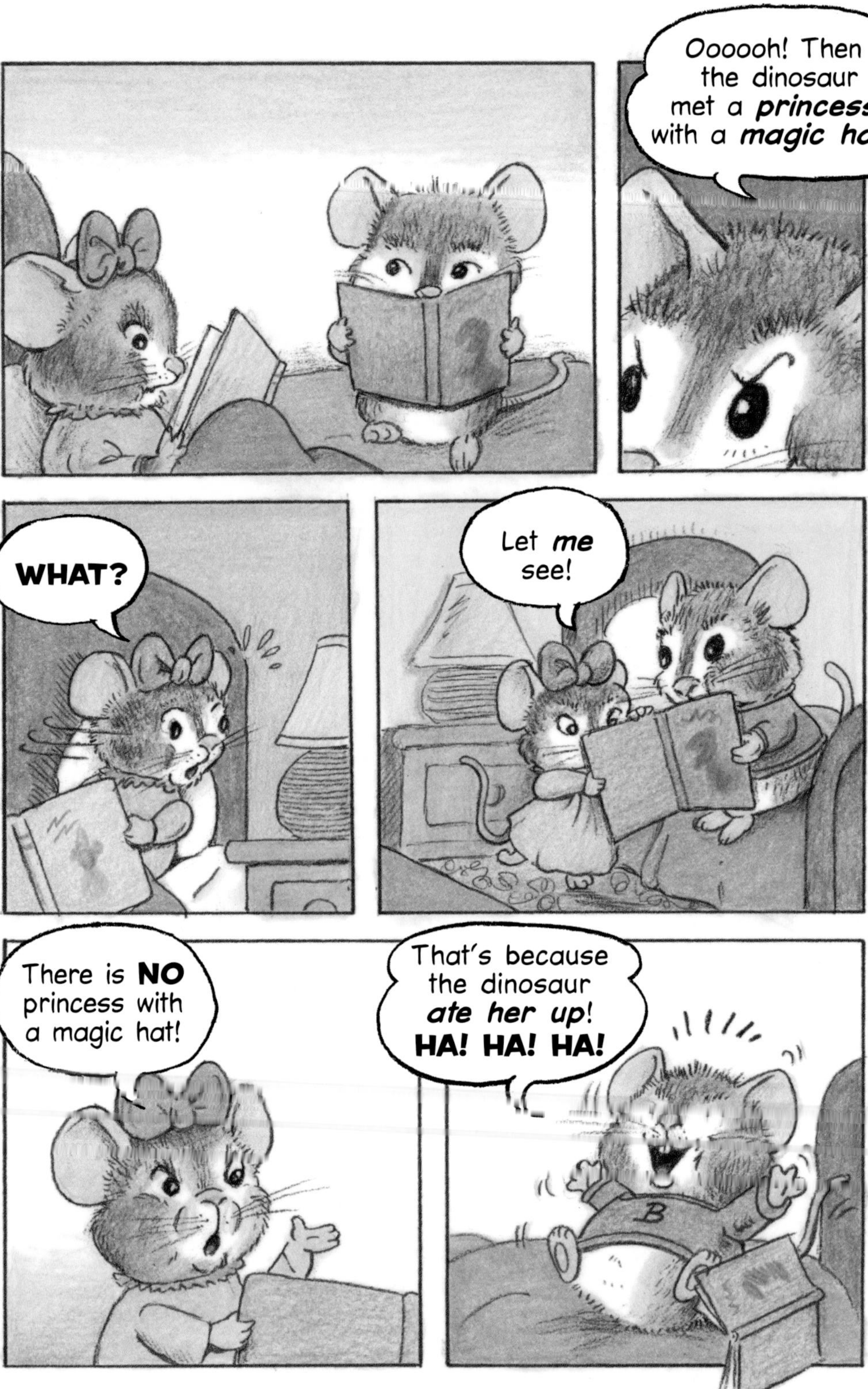
Oooooh! Then the dinosaur met a princess with a magic hat!
WHAT?
Let me see!
There is NO princess with a magic hat!
That's because the dinosaur ate her up! HA! HA! HA!

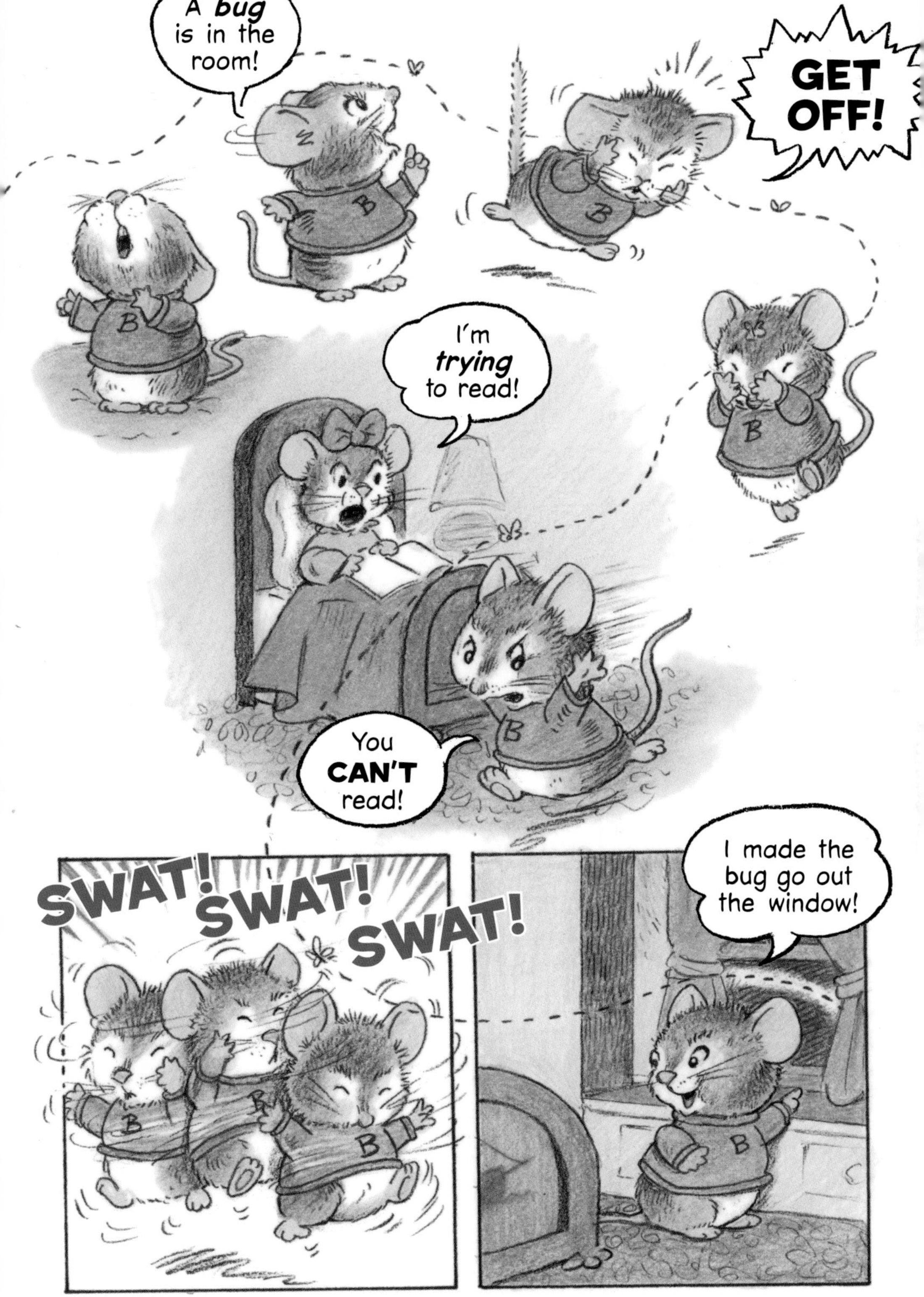
A **bug** is in the room!
GET OFF!
I'm ***trying*** to read!
You **CAN'T** read!
SWAT! SWAT! SWAT!
I made the bug go out the window!

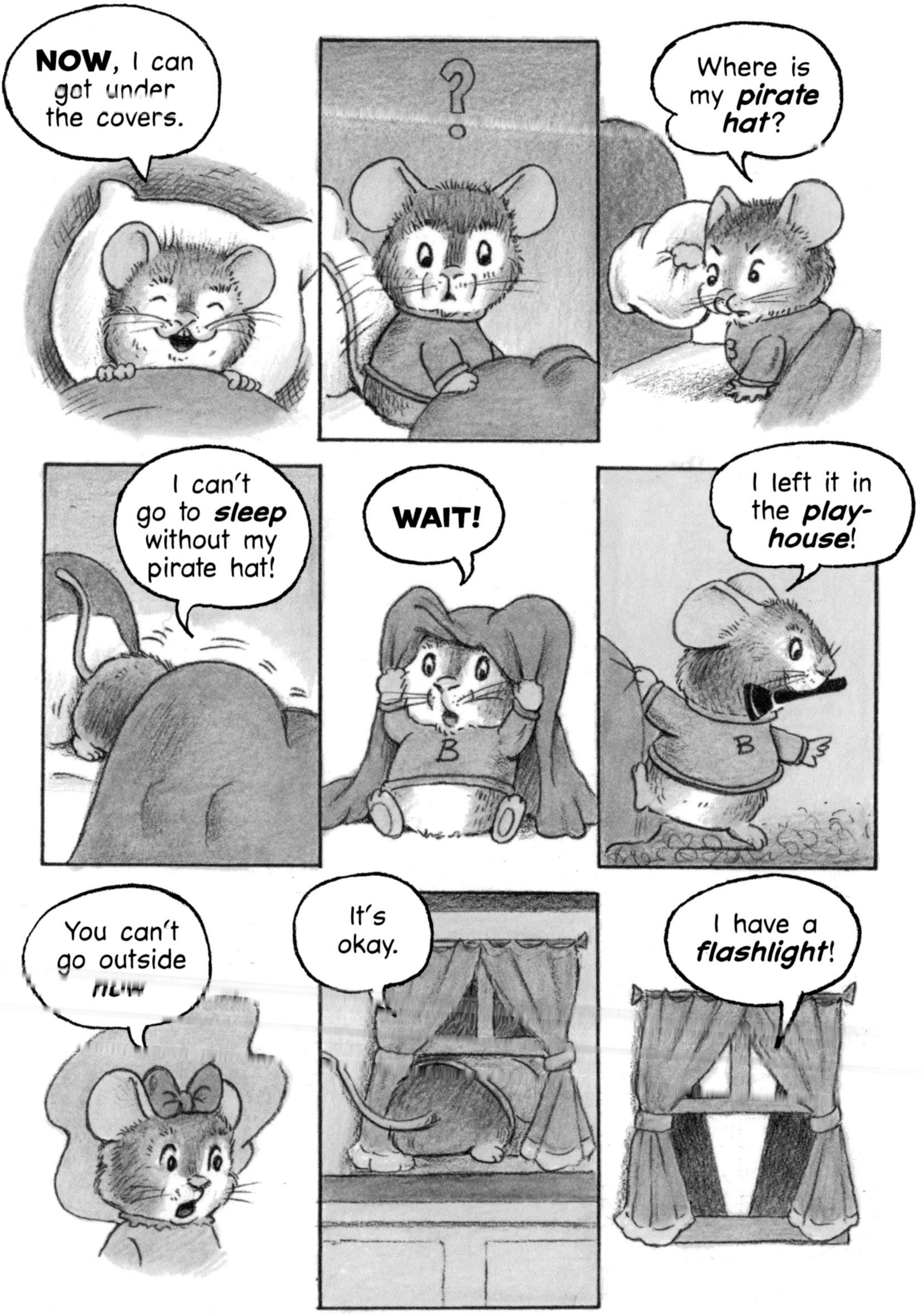
NOW, I can got under the covers.
?
Where is my ***pirate hat***?
I can't go to ***sleep*** without my pirate hat!
WAIT!
I left it in the ***play-house***!
You can't go outside
It's okay.
I have a ***flashlight***!

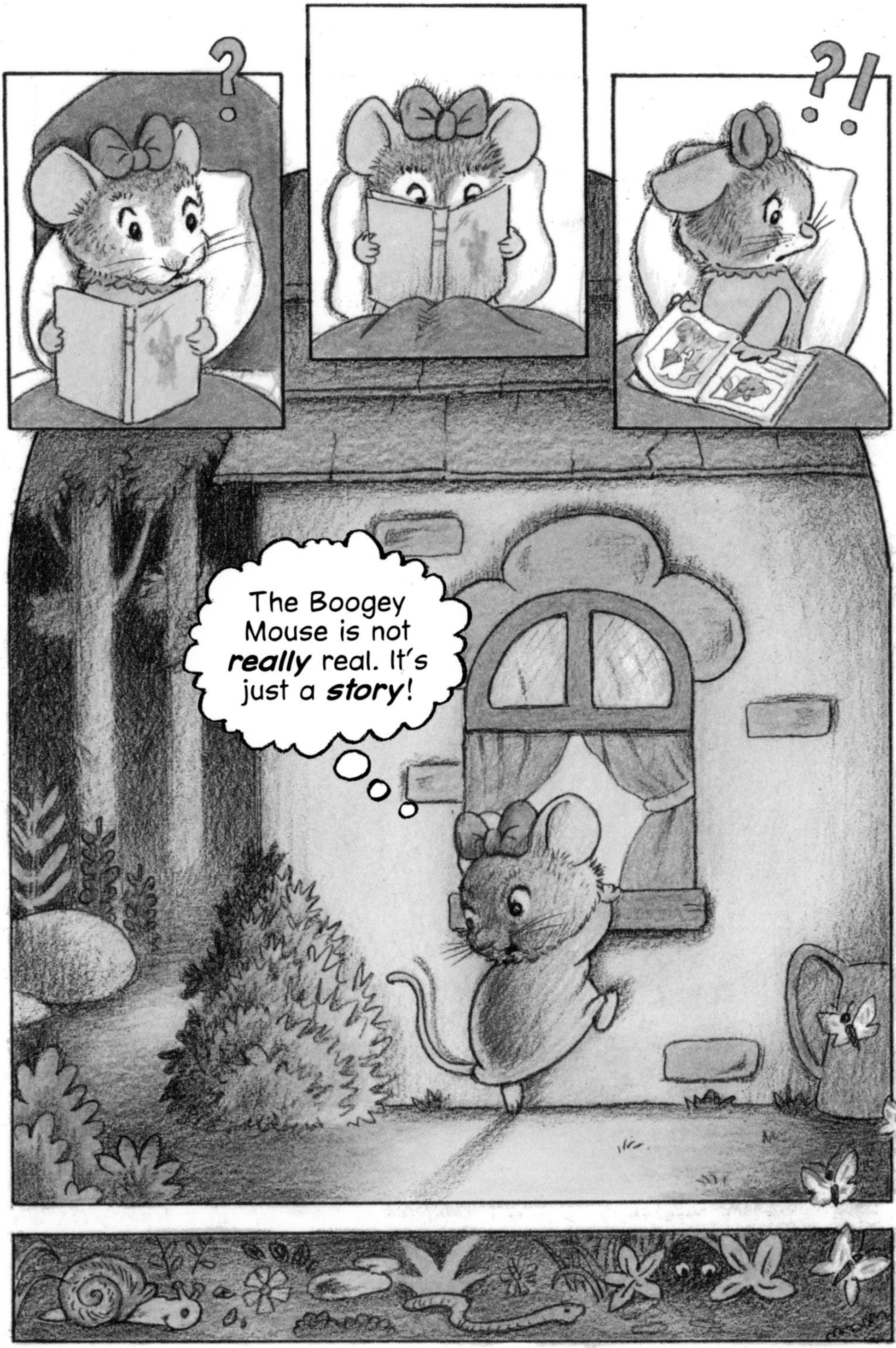
?
?!
The Boogey Mouse is not *really* real. It's just a *story*!

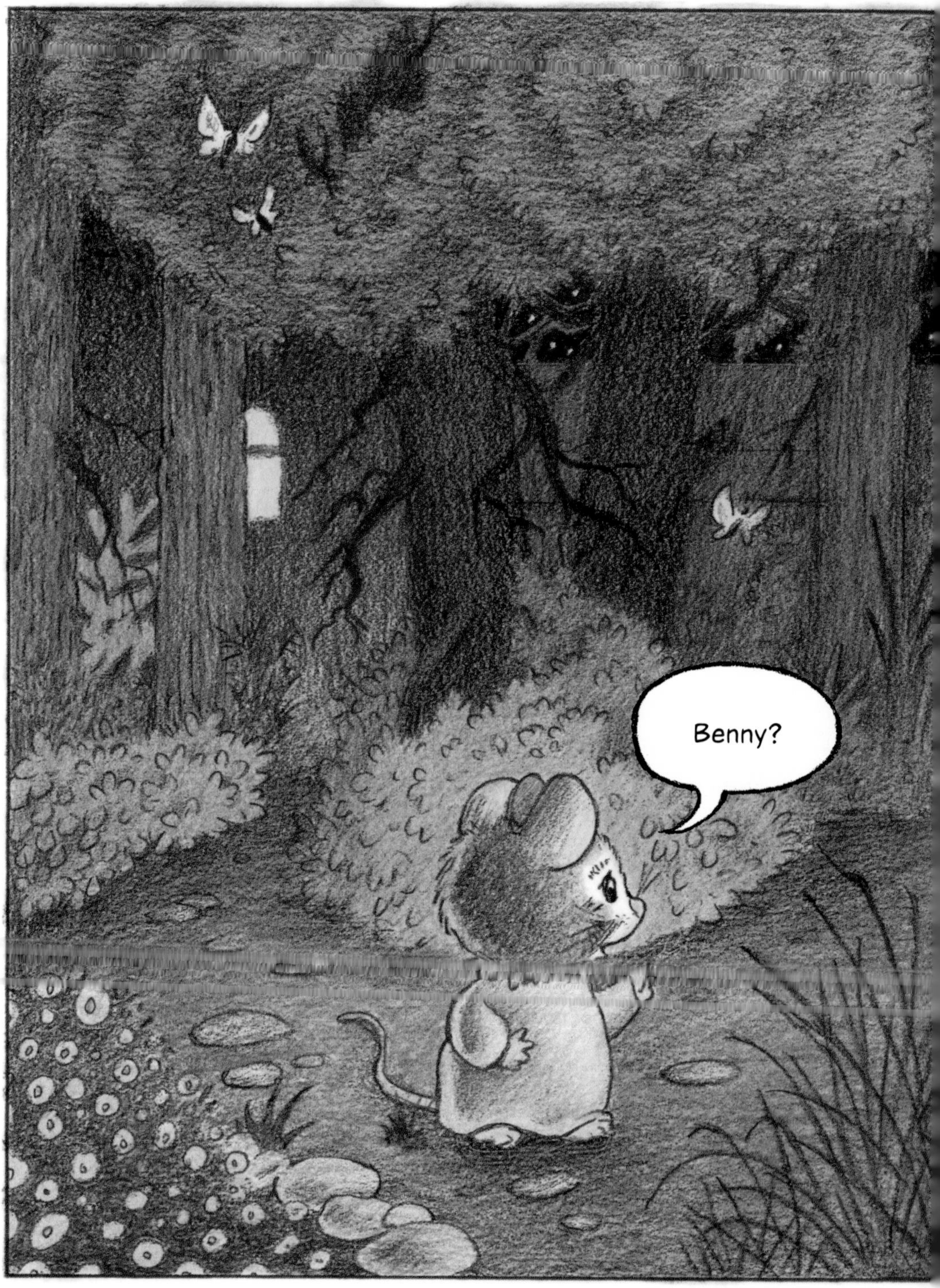
Benny?

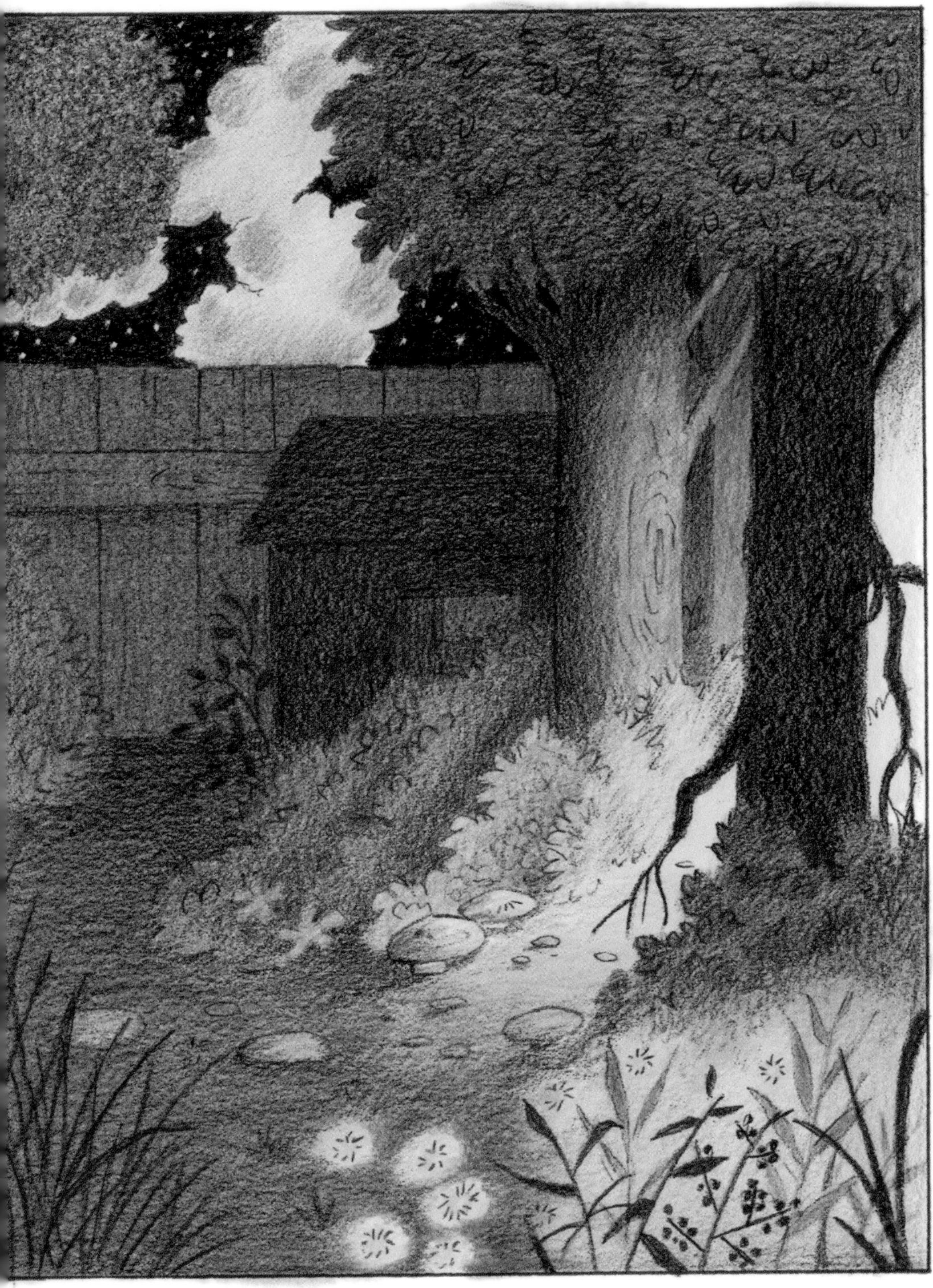

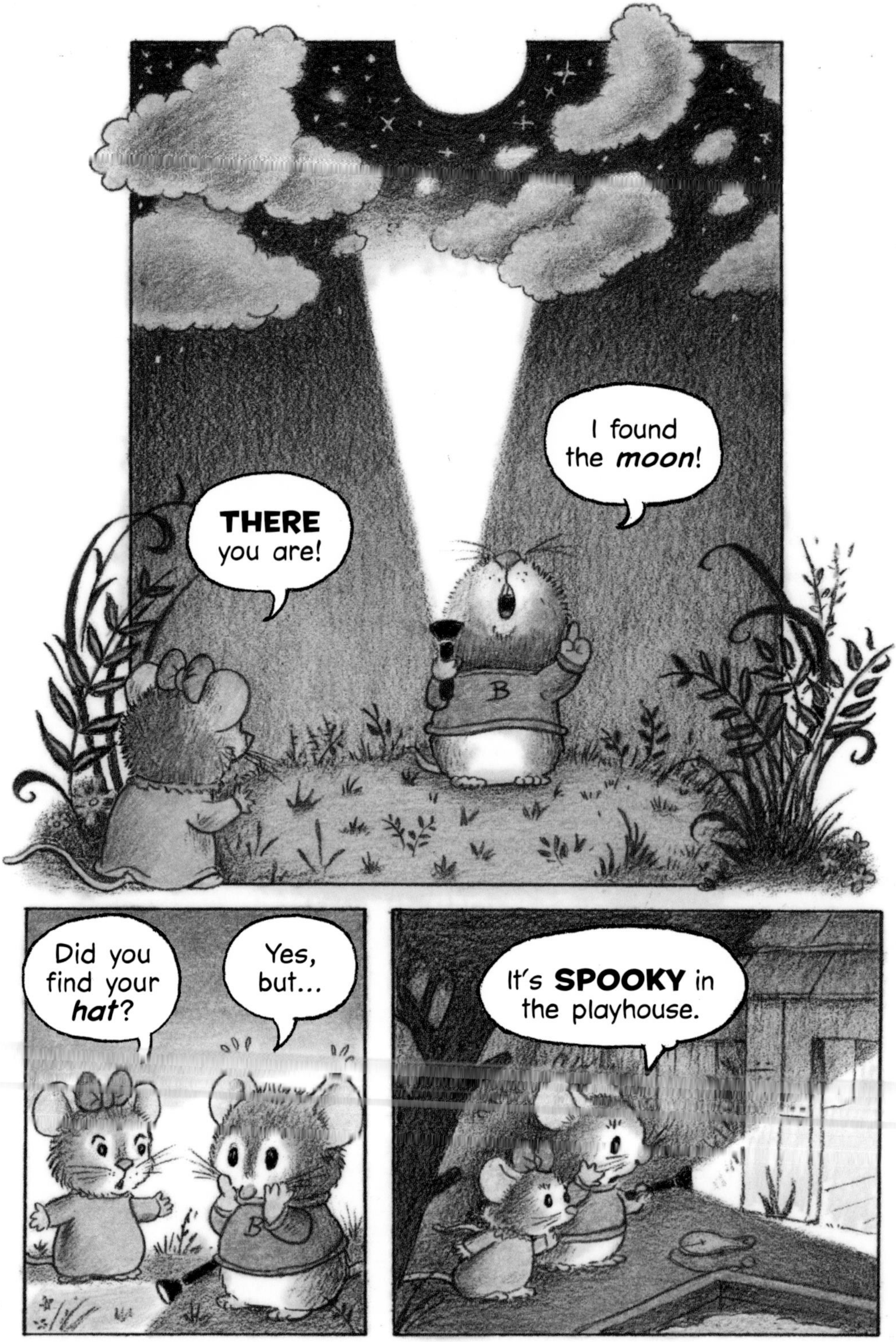
I found the *moon*!
THERE you are!
Did you find your *hat*?
Yes, but...
It's **SPOOKY** in the playhouse.

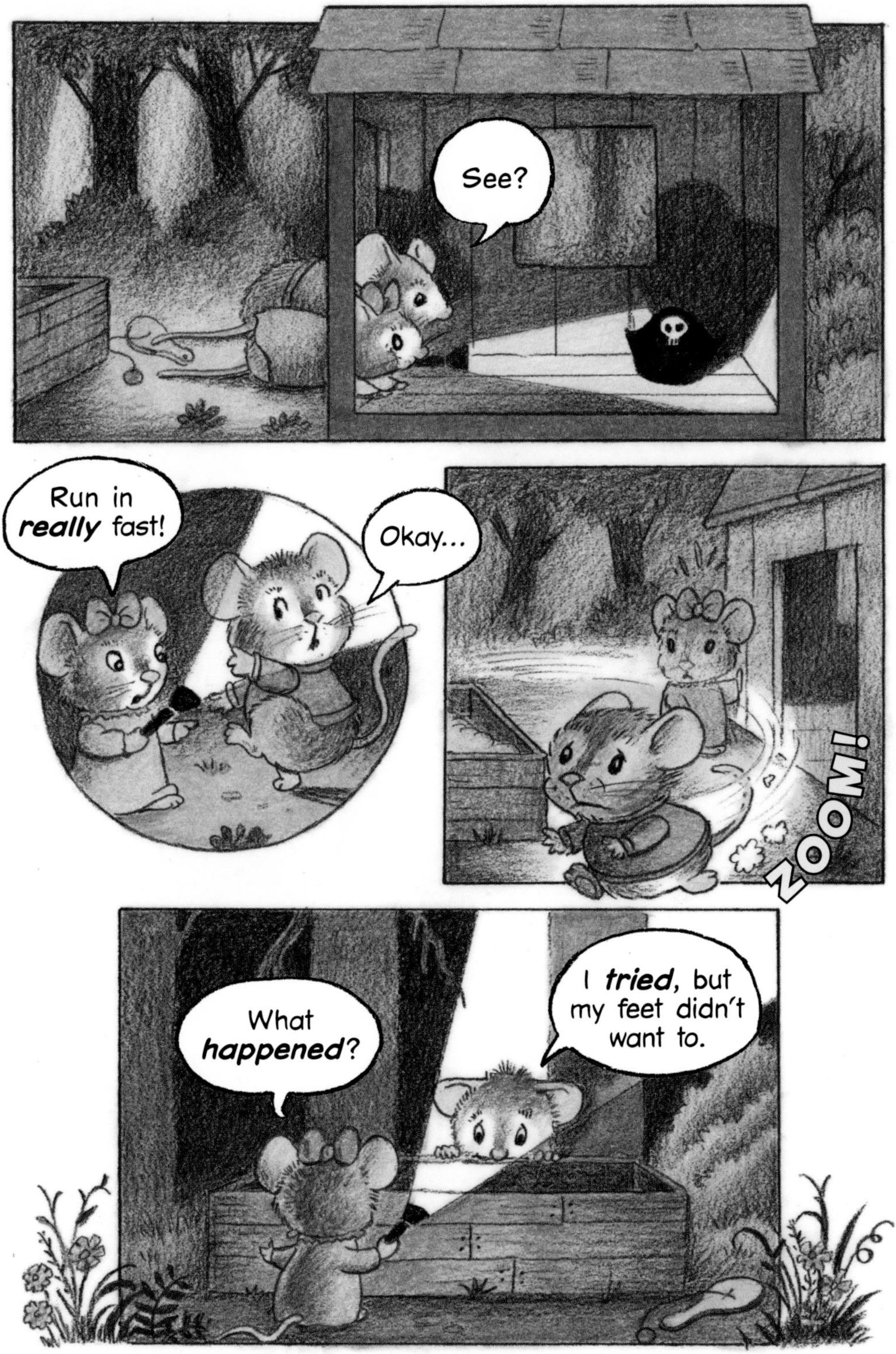
See?
Run in ***really*** fast!
Okay...
ZOOM!
What ***happened***?
I ***tried***, but my feet didn't want to.

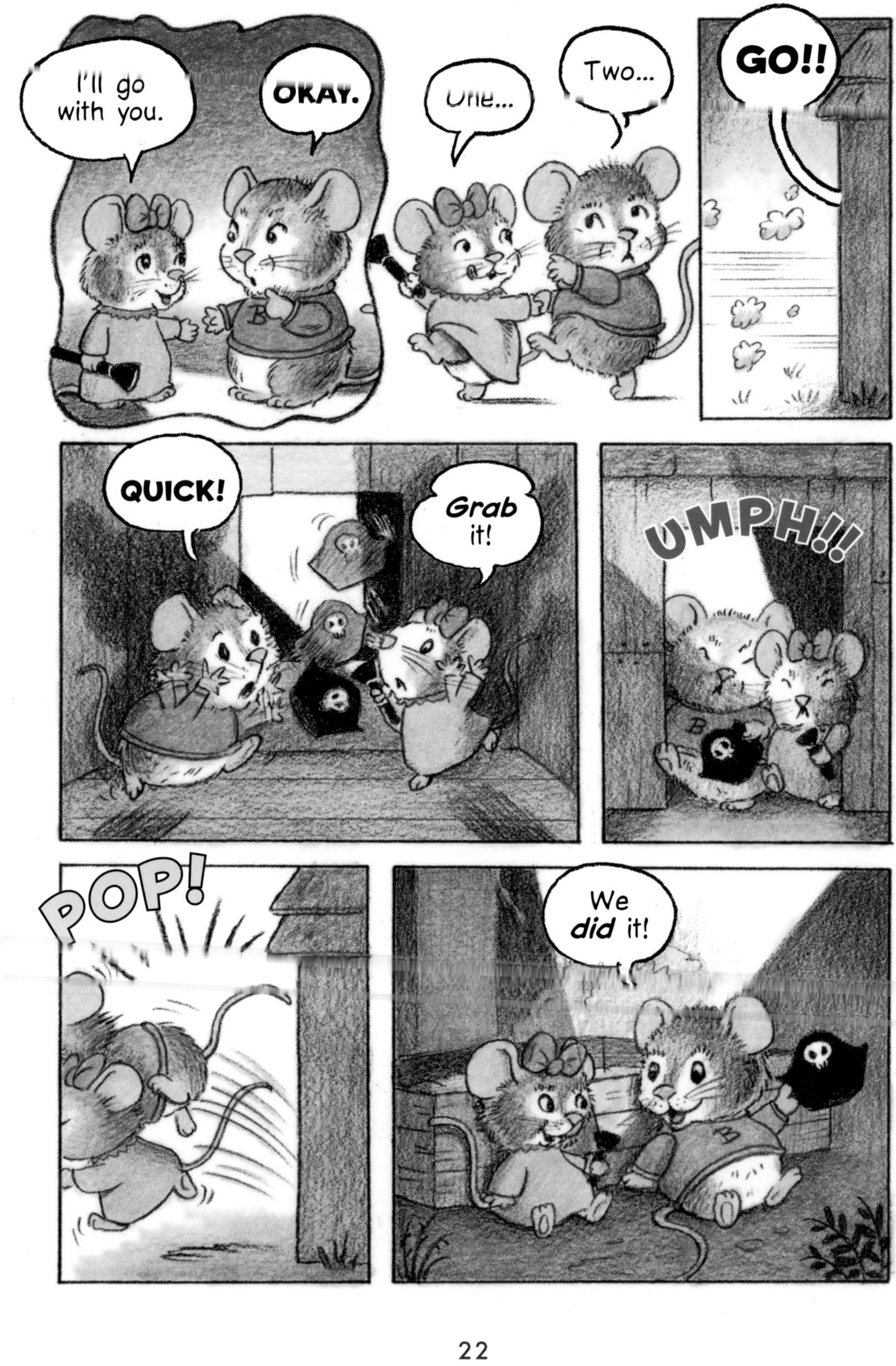
I'll go with you.
OKAY.
One...
Two...
GO!!
QUICK!
Grab it!
UMPH!!
POP!
We did it!

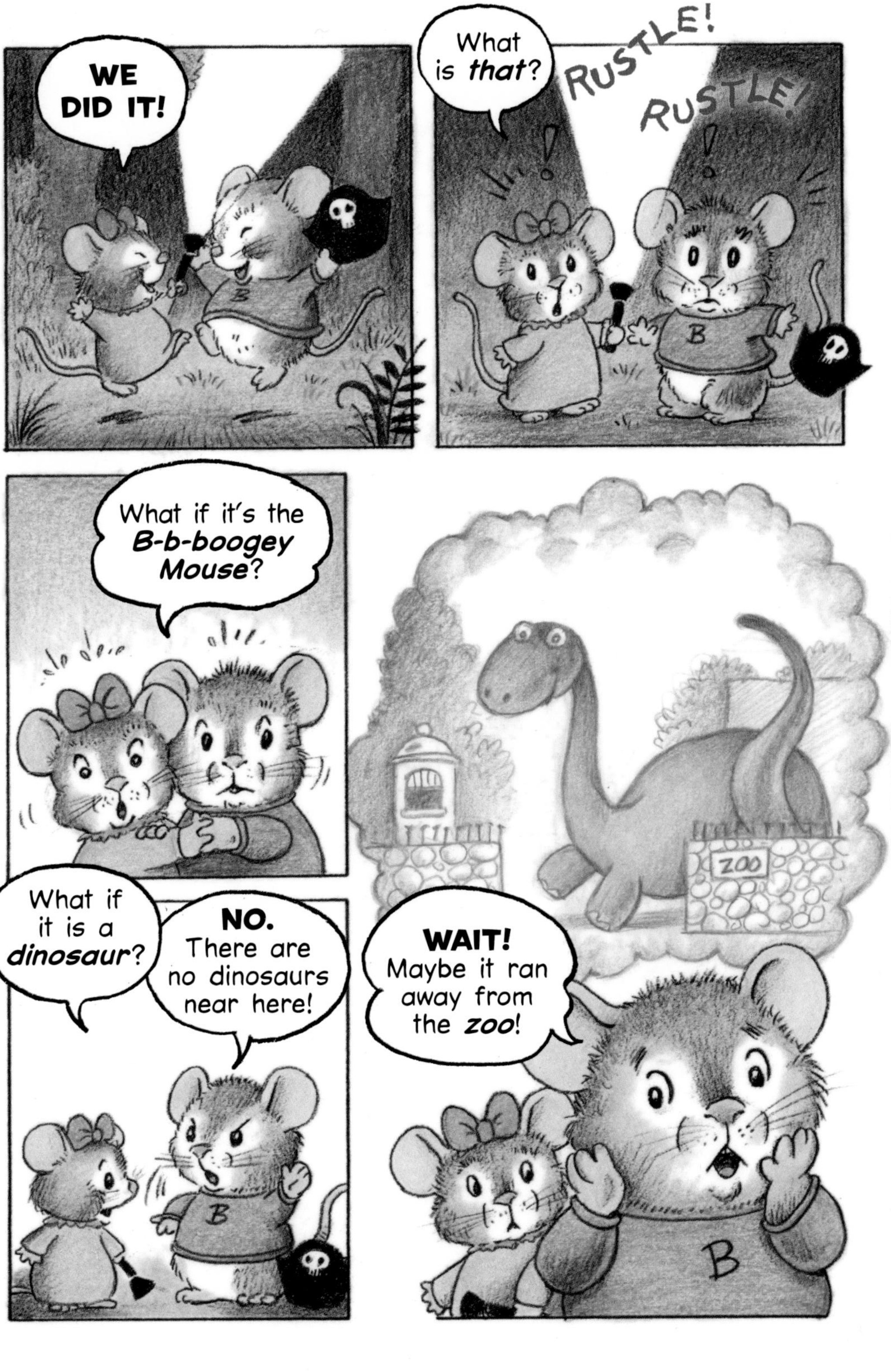
WE DID IT!
What is *that*?
RUSTLE!
RUSTLE!
What if it's the *B-b-boogey Mouse*?
What if it is a *dinosaur*?
NO. There are no dinosaurs near here!
ZOO
WAIT! Maybe it ran away from the *zoo*!

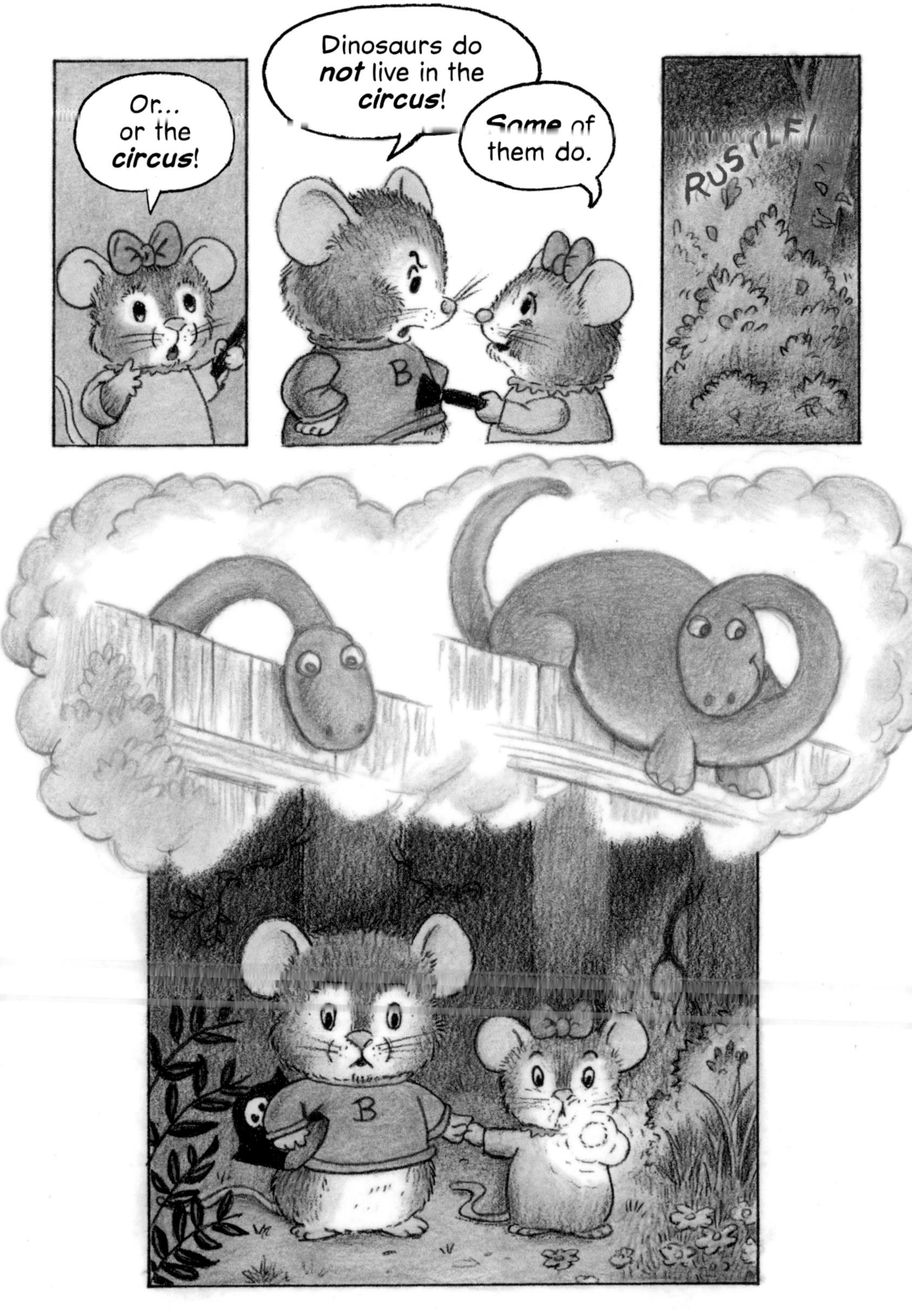
Or...
or the
circus!
Dinosaurs do
not live in the
circus!
Some of
them do.
RUSTLE!

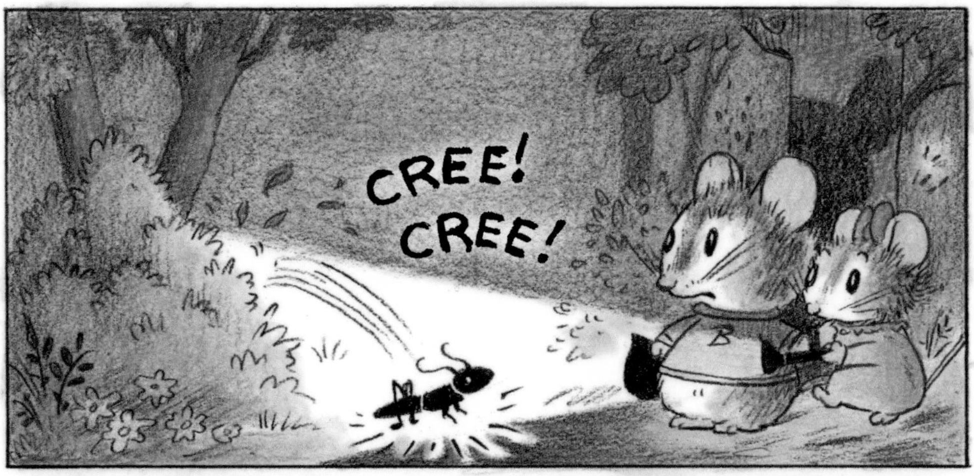
CREE!
CREE!
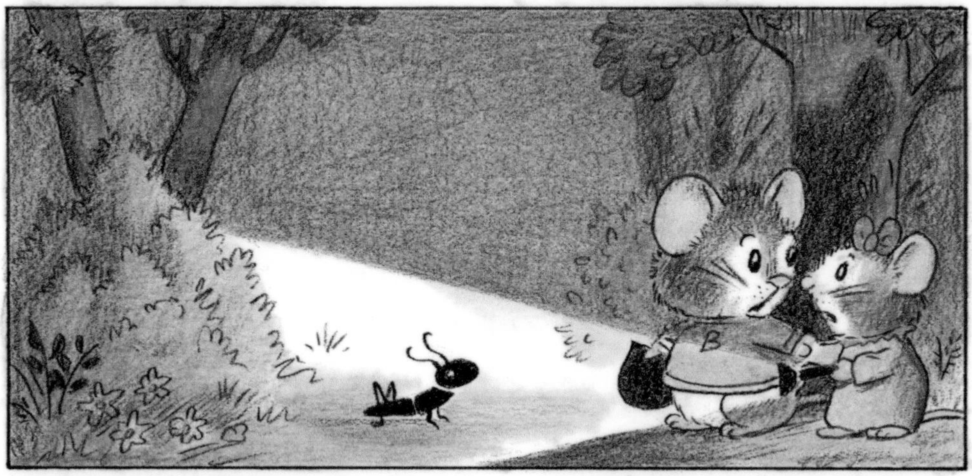
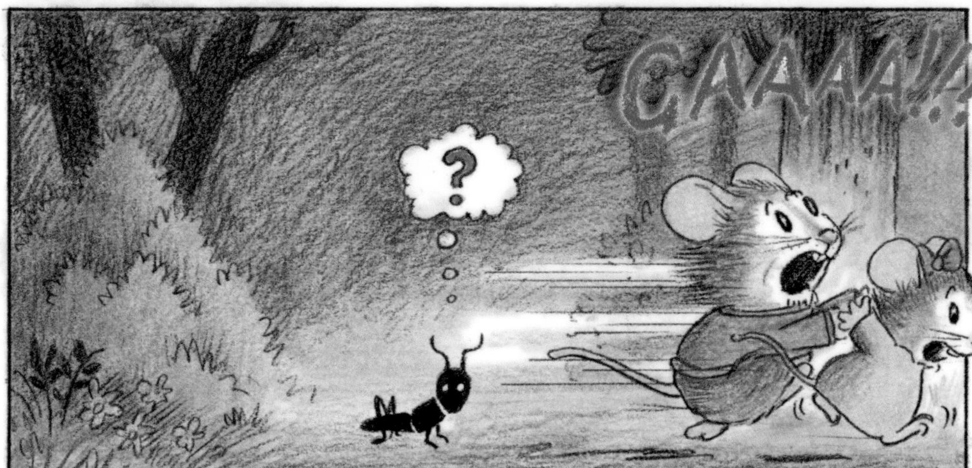
?
GAAAA!!!

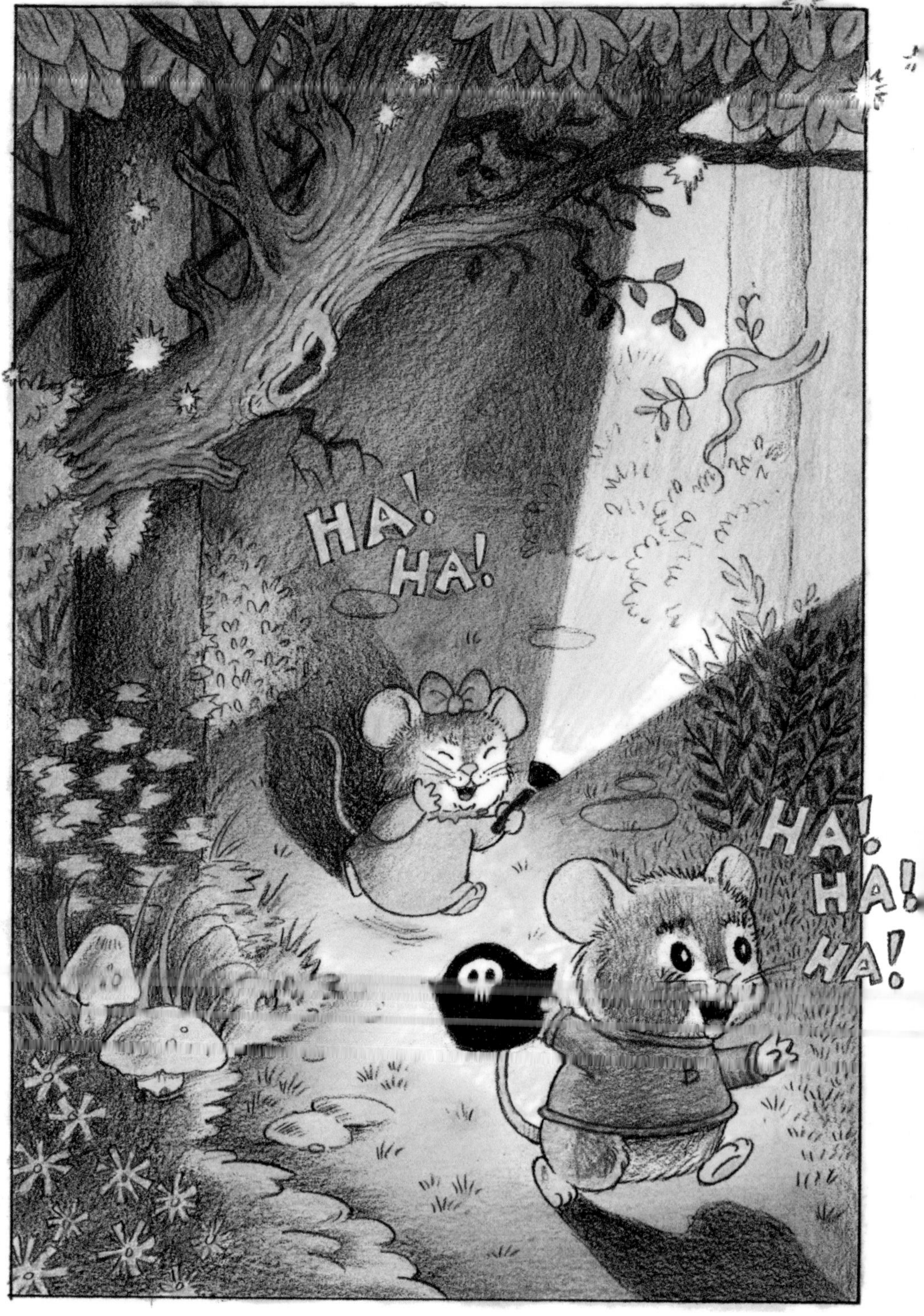
HA!
HA!
HA!
HA!
HA!

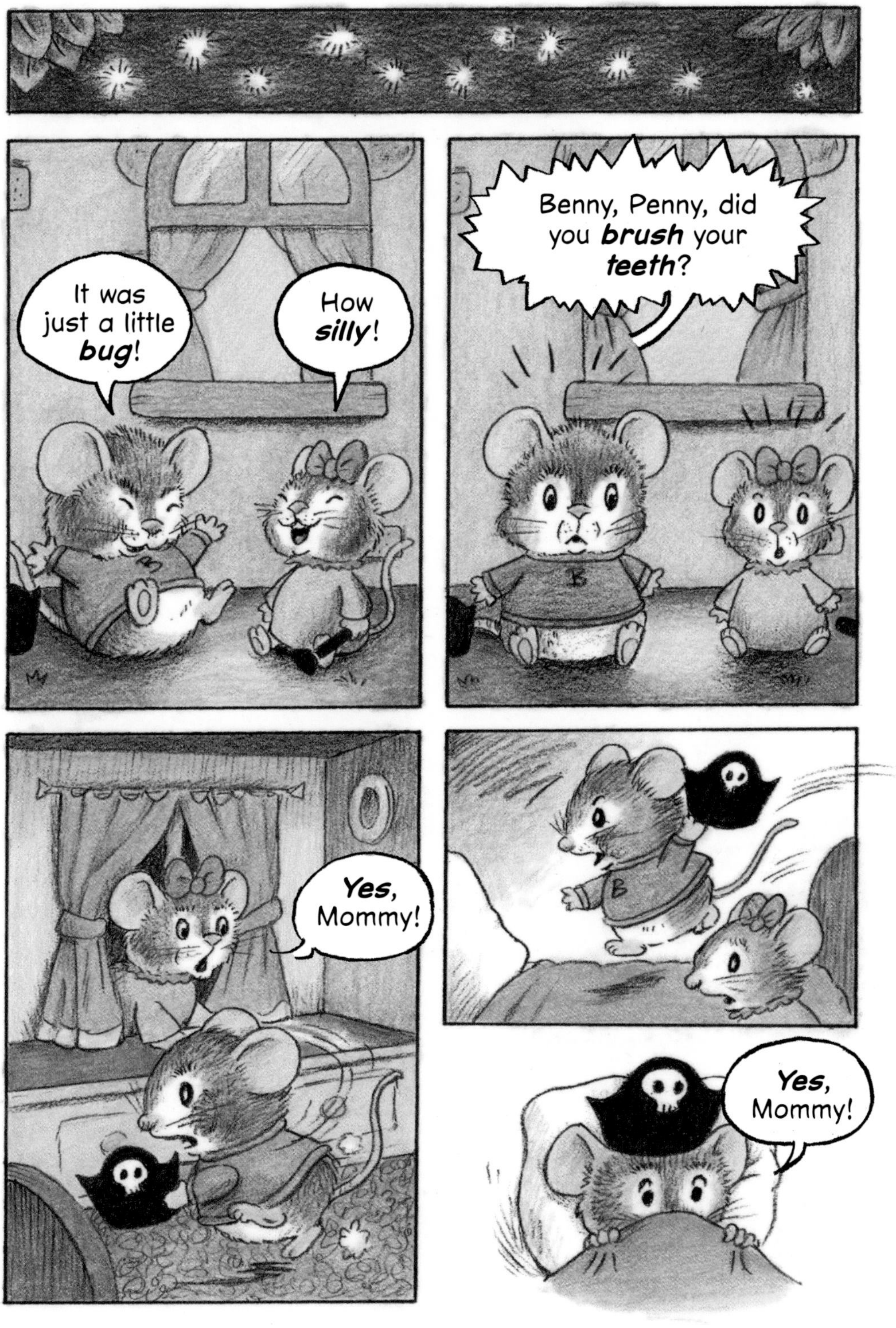
It was just a little bug!
How silly!
Benny, Penny, did you brush your teeth?
Yes, Mommy!
Yes, Mommy!

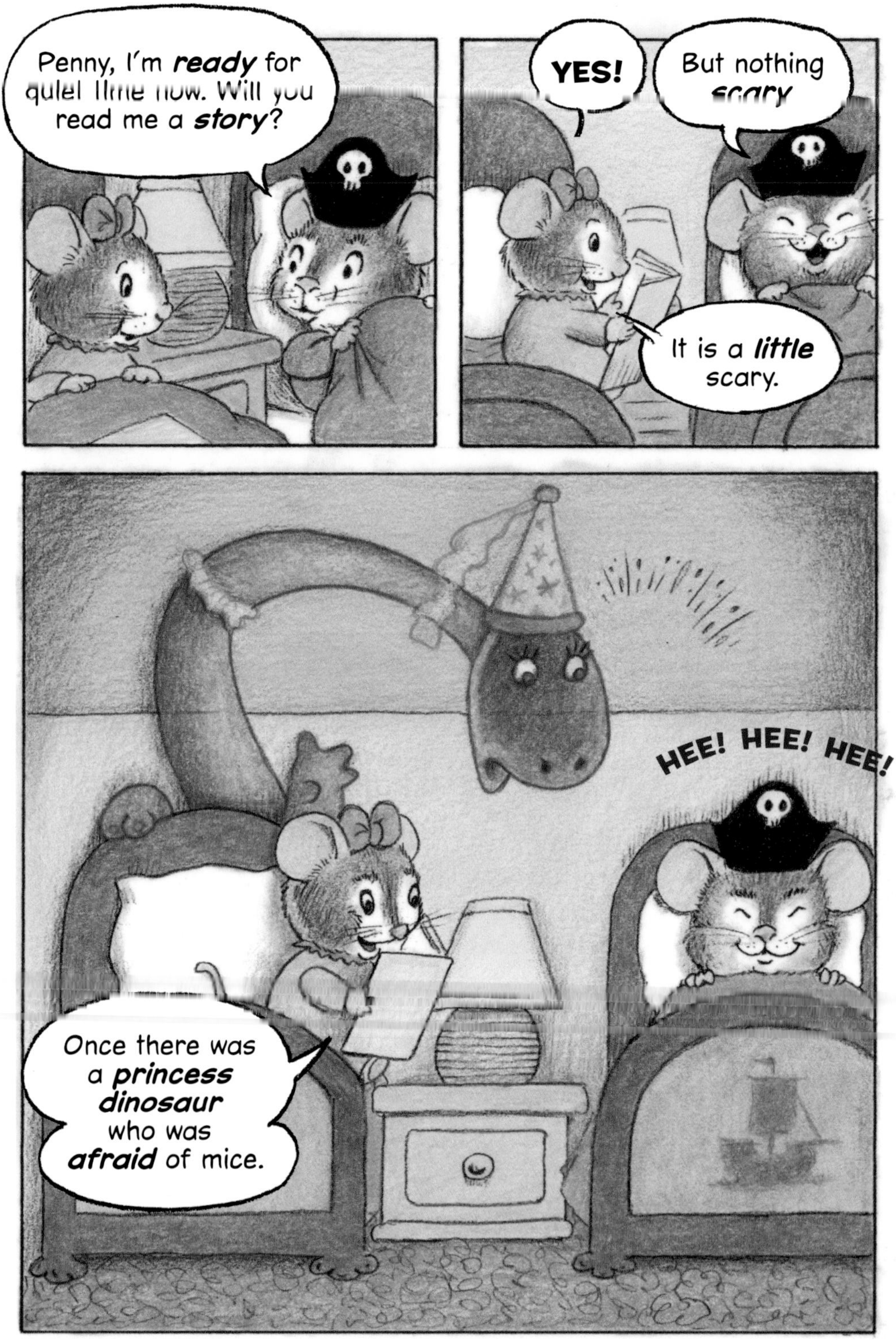
Penny, I'm ready for quiet time now. Will you read me a story?
YES!
But nothing scary
It is a little scary.
HEE! HEE! HEE!
Once there was a princess dinosaur who was afraid of mice.

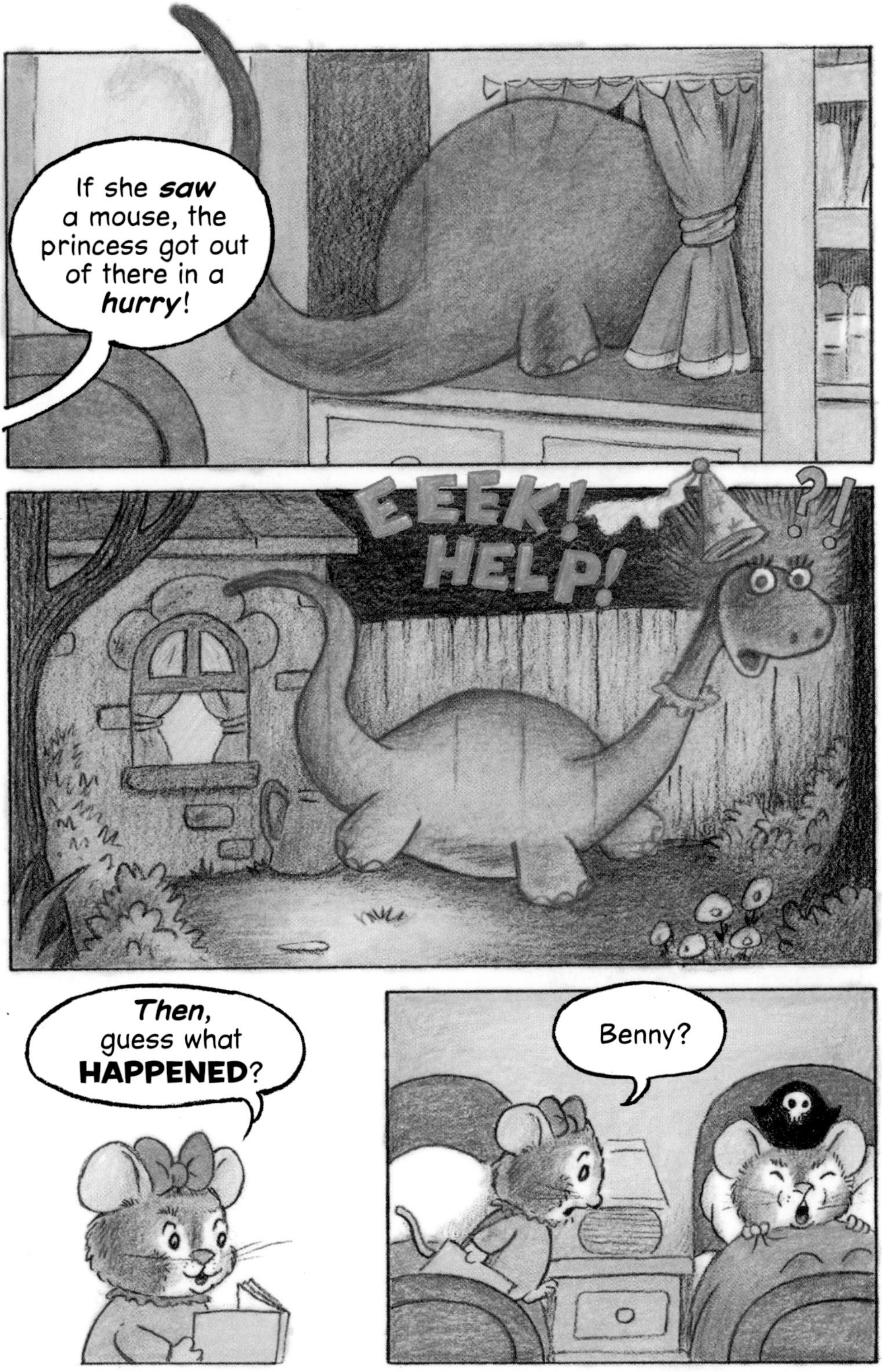

If she *saw* a mouse, the princess got out of there in a *hurry*!
EEEK! HELP!
?!
Then, guess what **HAPPENED**?
Benny?

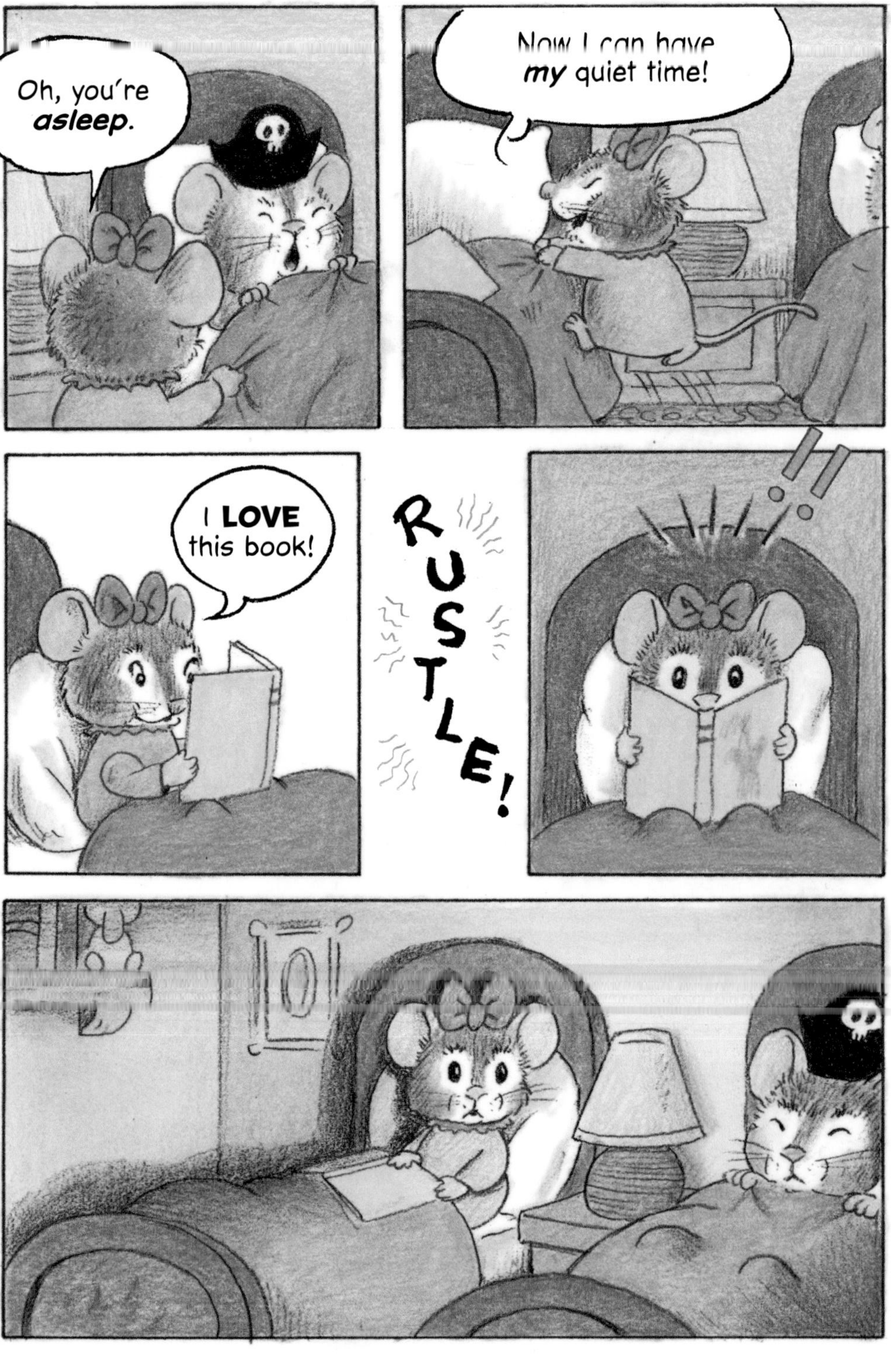
Oh, you're *asleep*.
Now I can have *my* quiet time!
I **LOVE** this book!
RUSTLE!
!!

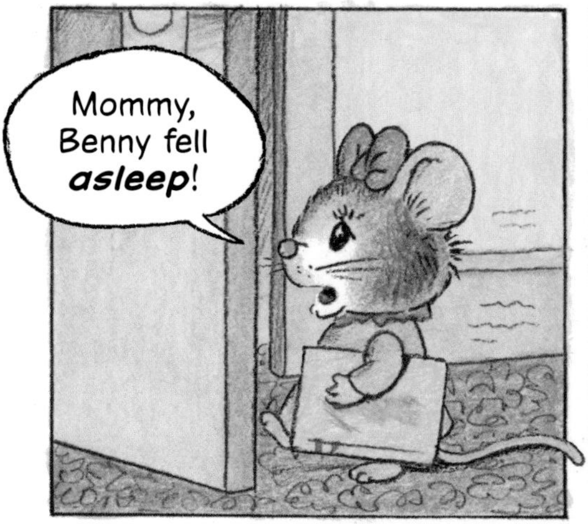
Mommy, Benny fell **asleep**!

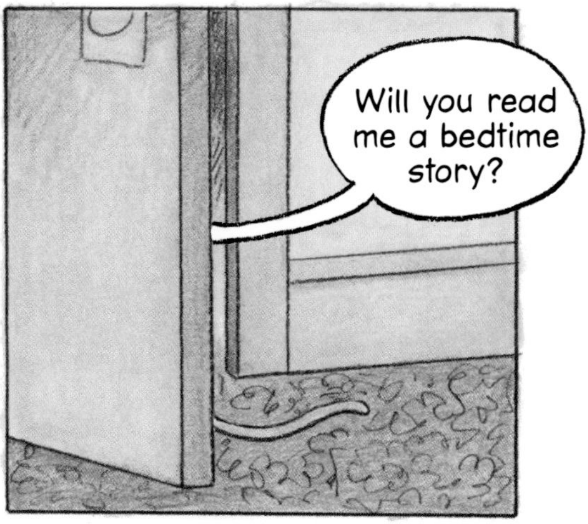
Will you read me a bedtime story?

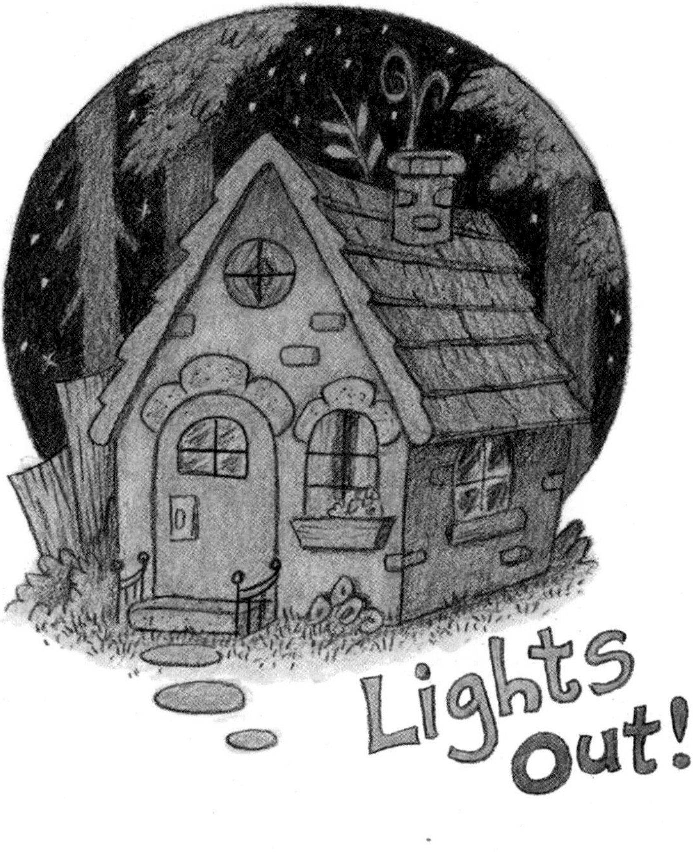
Lights out!

ABOUT THE AUTHOR

GEOFFREY HAYES has written and illustrated over forty children's books, including the extremely popular series of early readers *Otto and Uncle Tooth*, the classic *Bear by Himself*, and, most recently, *The Bunny's Night Light: A Glow-In-The-Dark Search*. His Benny and Penny titles for TOON Books are bestsellers and have garnered multiple awards. In 2010, *Benny and Penny in the Big No-No!* received the prestigious Theodor Seuss Geisel Award, given to the "most distinguished book for beginning readers published during the preceding year." When Geoffrey was younger, his flashlight was his favorite toy.

Geoffrey says, "My flashlight had red, green and blue filters that could be turned to change the color of the light. I used it to put on puppet plays starring my stuffed animals."

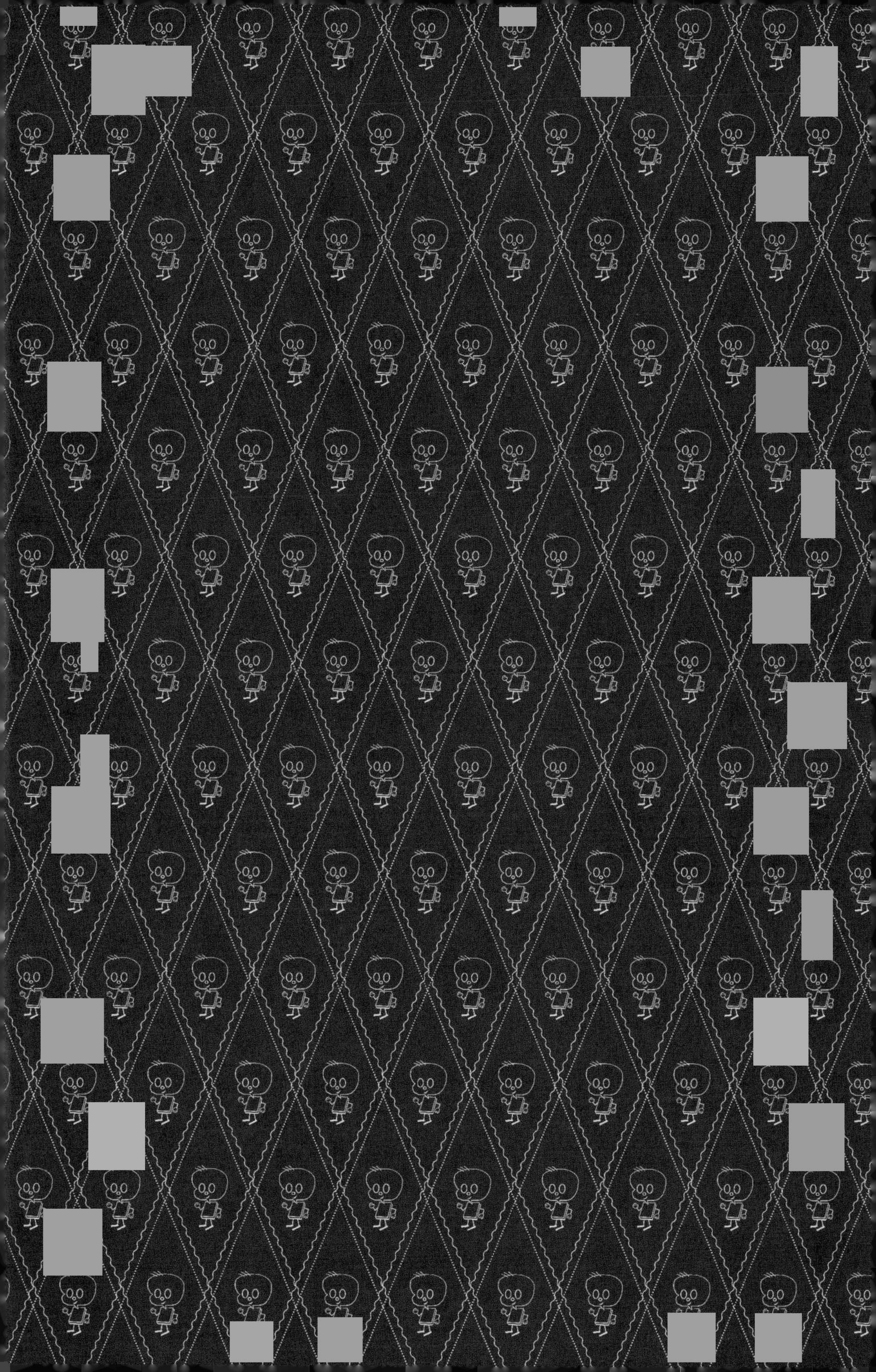

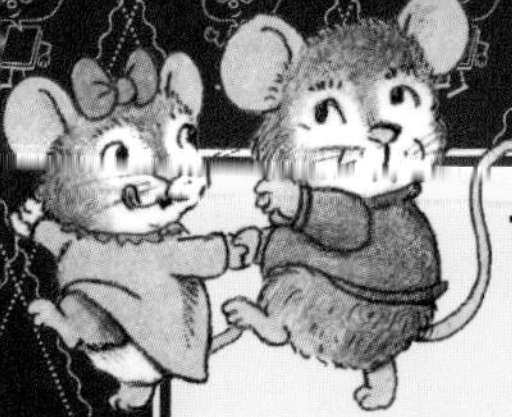

TIPS FOR PARENTS AND TEACHERS:

HOW TO READ COMICS WITH KIDS

Kids *love* comics! They are naturally drawn to the details in the pictures, which make them want to read the words. Comics beg for repeated readings and let both emerging and reluctant readers enjoy complex stories with a rich vocabulary. But since comics have their own grammar, here are a few tips for reading them with kids:

GUIDE YOUNG READERS: Use your finger to show your place in the text, but keep it at the bottom of the speaking character so it doesn't hide the very important facial expressions.

HAM IT UP! Think of the comic book story as a play and don't hesitate to read with expression and intonation. Assign parts or get kids to supply the sound effects, a great way to reinforce phonics skills.

LET THEM GUESS. Comics provide lots of context for the words, so emerging readers can make informed guesses. Like jigsaw puzzles, comics ask readers to make connections, so check a young audience's understanding by asking, "What's this character thinking?" (but don't be surprised if a kid finds some of the comics' subtle details faster than you).

TALK ABOUT THE PICTURES. Point out how the artist paces the story with pauses (silent panels) or speeded-up action (a burst of short panels). Discuss how the size and shape of the panels carry meaning.

ABOVE ALL, ENJOY! There is of course never one right way to read, so go for the shared pleasure. Once children make the story happen in their imagination, they have discovered the thrill of reading, and you won't be able to stop them. At that point, just go get them more books, and more comics.

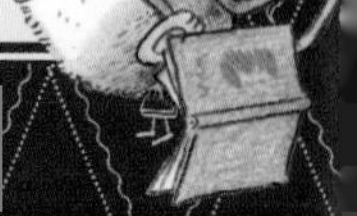

TOON INTO READING

LEVEL 1

GRADES K–1

LEXILE BR–100 • GUIDED READING E–G • READING RECOVERY 7–10

FIRST COMICS FOR BRAND-NEW READERS

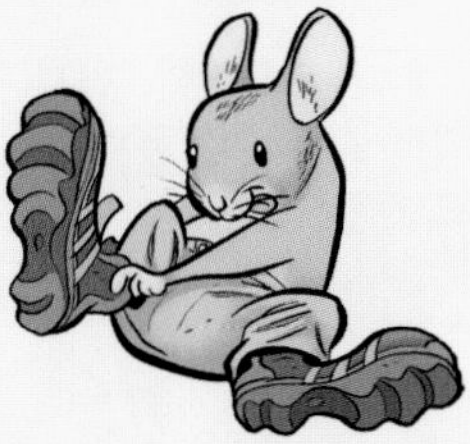

- 200–300 easy sight words
- short sentences
- often one character
- single time frame or theme
- 1–2 panels per page

LEVEL 2

GRADES 1–2

LEXILE BR–170 • GUIDED READING G–J • READING RECOVERY 11–17

EASY-TO-READ COMICS FOR EMERGING READERS

- 300–600 words
- short sentences and repetition
- story arc with few characters in a small world
- 1–4 panels per page

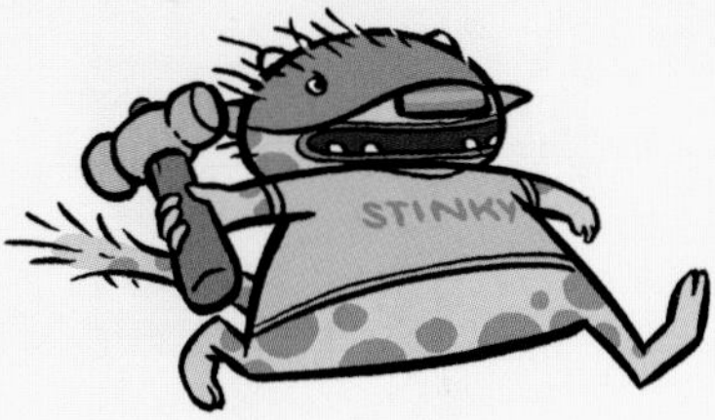
STINKY

LEVEL 3

GRADES 2–3

LEXILE 150–300 • GUIDED READING J–N • READING RECOVERY 17–19

CHAPTER-BOOK COMICS FOR ADVANCED BEGINNERS

- 800–1000+ words in long sentences
- broad world as well as shifts in time and place
- long story divided in chapters
- reader needs to make connections and speculate

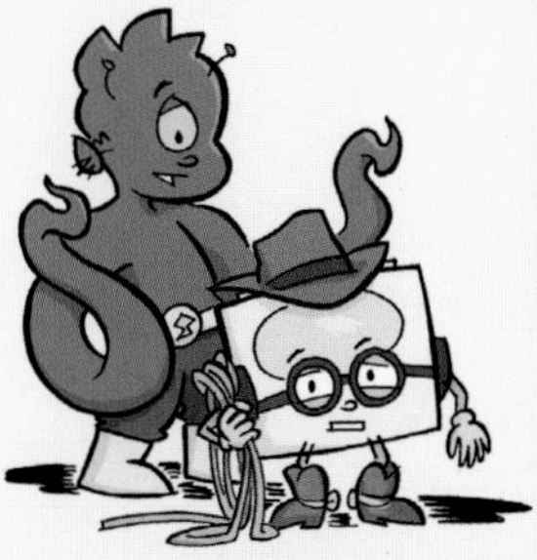

COLLECT THEM ALL!

LEVEL 1 FIRST COMICS FOR BRAND-NEW READERS

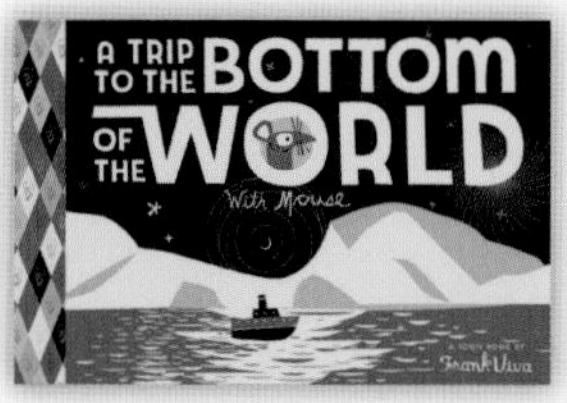
A TRIP TO THE BOTTOM OF THE WORLD
With Mouse
Frank Viva

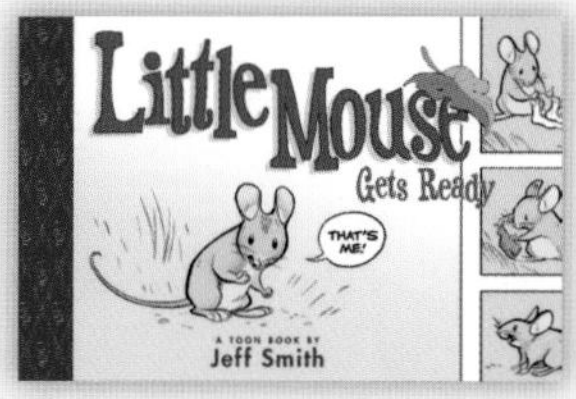
Little Mouse Gets Ready
THAT'S ME!
A TOON BOOK BY
Jeff Smith

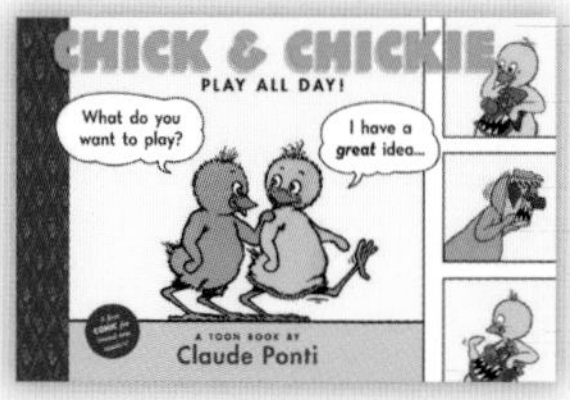
CHICK & CHICKIE
PLAY ALL DAY!
What do you want to play?
I have a great idea...
A TOON BOOK BY
Claude Ponti

LEVEL 2 EASY-TO-READ COMICS FOR EMERGING READERS

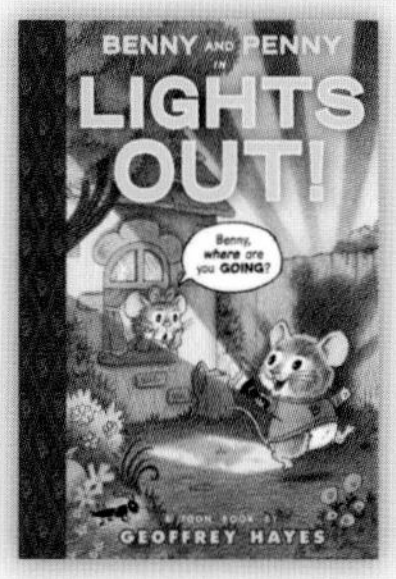
BENNY AND PENNY IN
LIGHTS OUT!
Benny, where are you GOING?
GEOFFREY HAYES

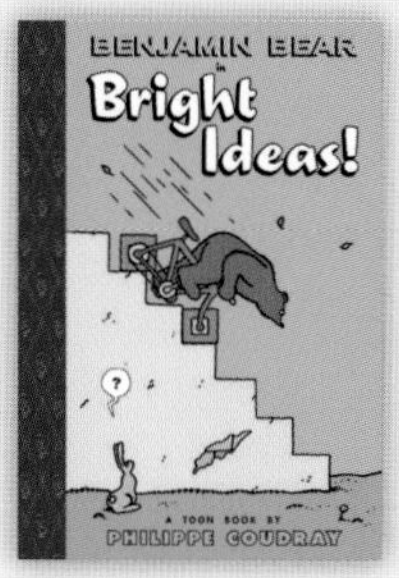
BENJAMIN BEAR IN
Bright Ideas!
A TOON BOOK BY
PHILIPPE COUDRAY

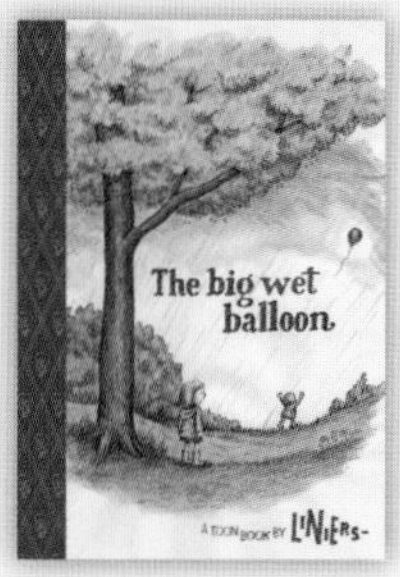
The big wet balloon
A TOON BOOK BY LINIERS

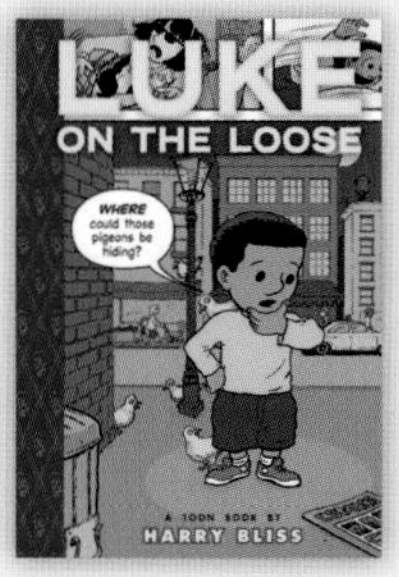
LUKE ON THE LOOSE
WHERE could those pigeons be hiding?
A TOON BOOK BY
HARRY BLISS

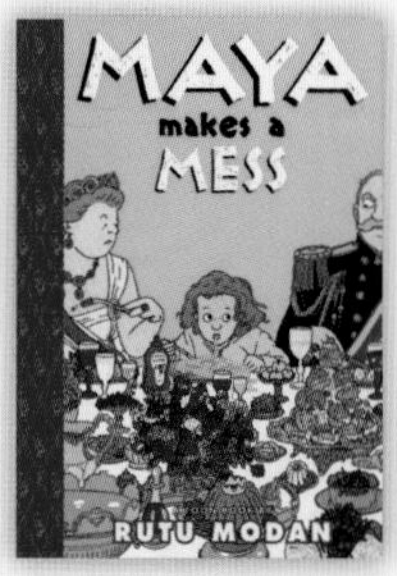
MAYA makes a MESS
RUTU MODAN

LEVEL 3 CHAPTER-BOOK COMICS FOR ADVANCED BEGINNERS

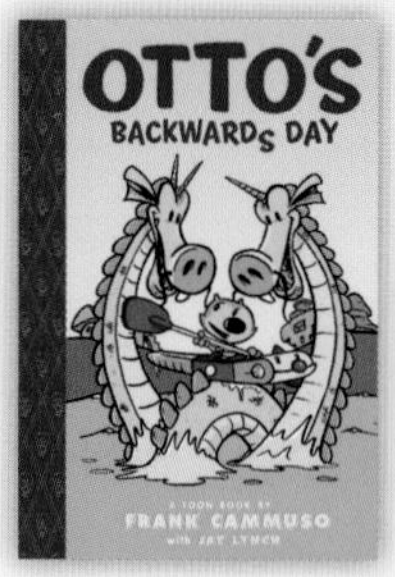
OTTO'S BACKWARDS DAY
A TOON BOOK BY
FRANK CAMMUSO
with JAY LYNCH

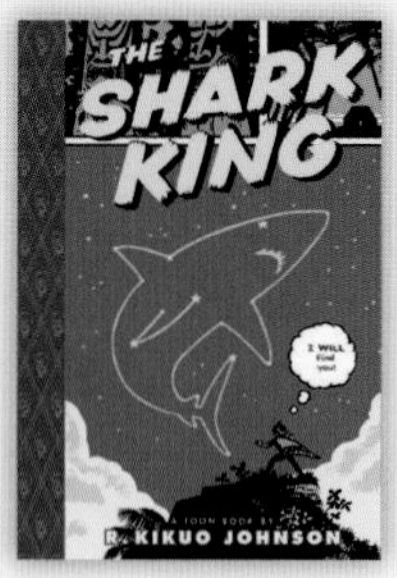
THE SHARK KING
I WILL find you!
A TOON BOOK BY
R. KIKUO JOHNSON

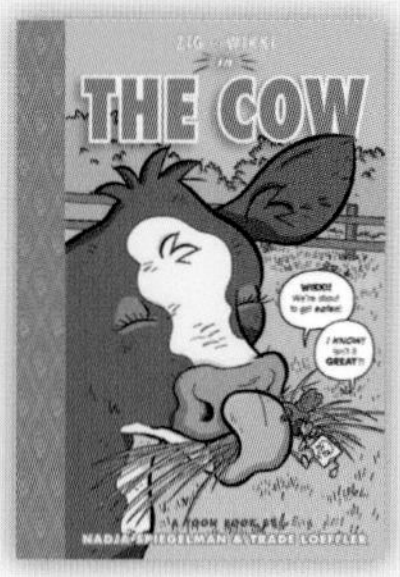
ZIG AND WIKKI IN
THE COW
NADJA SPIEGELMAN & TRADE LOEFFLER

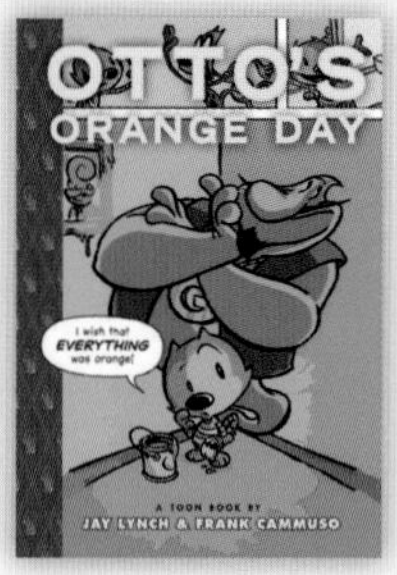
OTTO'S ORANGE DAY
I wish that EVERYTHING was orange!
A TOON BOOK BY
JAY LYNCH & FRANK CAMMUSO

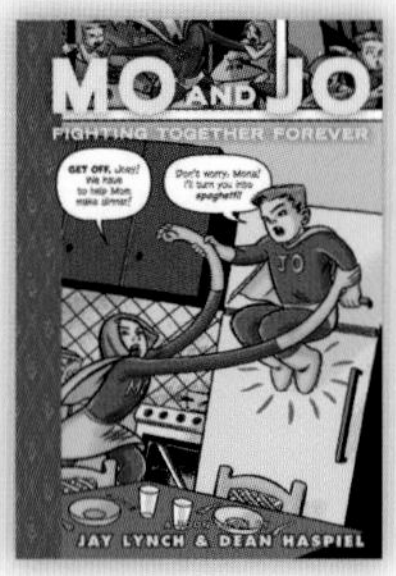
MO AND JO
FIGHTING TOGETHER FOREVER
JAY LYNCH & DEAN HASPIEL

TOON BOOKS

Set 1 • 10 hardcover books	**978-1-61479-147-8**
Benny and Penny in Just Pretend	978-1-61479-148-5
Benny and Penny in the Toy Breaker	978-1-61479-149-2
Chick & Chickie Play All Day!	978-1-61479-150-8
Jack and the Box	978-1-61479-151-5
Mo and Jo Fighting Together Forever	978-1-61479-152-2
Nina in That Makes Me Mad!	978-1-61479-153-9
Otto's Orange Day	978-1-61479-154-6
Silly Lilly and the Four Seasons	978-1-61479-155-3
Silly Lilly in What Will I Be Today?	978-1-61479-156-0
Zig and Wikki in Something Ate My Homework	978-1-61479-157-7
Set 2 • 8 hardcover books	**978-1-61479-298-7**
Benjamin Bear in Fuzzy Thinking	978-1-61479-299-4
Benny and Penny in the Big No-No!	978-1-61479-300-7
Little Mouse Gets Ready	978-1-61479-301-4
Luke on the Loose	978-1-61479-302-1
Maya Makes a Mess	978-1-61479-303-8
Patrick in a Teddy Bear's Picnic and Other Stories	978-1-61479-304-5
The Shark King	978-1-61479-305-2
Zig and Wikki in the Cow	978-1-61479-306-9
Set 3 • 6 hardcover books	**978-1-61479-422-6**
Benjamin Bear in Bright Ideas!	978-1-61479-423-3
Benny and Penny in Lights Out!	978-1-61479-424-0
The Big Wet Balloon	978-1-61479-425-7
Otto's Backwards Day	978-1-61479-426-4
Patrick Eats His Peas and Other Stories	978-1-61479-427-1
A Trip to the Bottom of the World with Mouse	978-1-61479-428-8

9-16